MURDER AT THE HIGHLAND PRACTICE

Shortly after her return to the Scottish Highlands, DI Blair Hannah's small team of detectives is called upon to investigate a suspicious death in the rural town of Balloch Pass. The elderly woman had altered her will before she died, leaving everything to two unlikely beneficiaries: the local priest, and the town's new GP, Dr Noah Bradshaw. As Blair races against time to catch a potential killer, can she beat the ghosts of her past and grab the chance of her own happy ever after?

Books by Jo Bartlett
in the Linford Romance Library:

NO TIME FOR SECOND BEST
CHRISTMAS IN THE BAY
FALLING FOR DR. RIGHT
ST. FINBAR'S CROSS
ALWAYS THE BRIDESMAID
THE CHRISTMAS CHOIR

3 8015 02563 645 1

SPECIAL MESSAGE TO READERS

THE ULVERSCROFT FOUNDATION

(registered UK charity number 264873)

was established in 1972 to provide funds for research, diagnosis and treatment of eye diseases. Examples of major projects funded by the Ulverscroft Foundation are:-

- The Children's Eye Unit at Moorfields Eye Hospital, London
- The Ulverscroft Children's Eye Unit at Great Ormond Street Hospital for Sick Children
- Funding research into eye diseases and treatment at the Department of Ophthalmology, University of Leicester
- The Ulverscroft Vision Research Group, Institute of Child Health
- Twin operating theatres at the Western Ophthalmic Hospital, London
- The Chair of Ophthalmology at the Royal Australian College of Ophthalmologists

You can help further the work of the Foundation by making a donation or leaving a legacy. Every contribution is gratefully received. If you would like to help support the Foundation or require further information, please contact:

JO BARTLETT

MURDER AT THE HIGHLAND PRACTICE

Complete and Unabridged

LINFORD
Leicester

First published in Great Britain in 2018

First Linford Edition
published 2020

*A catalogue record for this book is available
from the British Library.*

ISBN 978–1–4448–4483–2

Published by
Ulverscroft Limited
Anstey, Leicestershire

Set by Words & Graphics Ltd.
Anstey, Leicestershire
Printed and bound in Great Britain by
T. J. International Ltd., Padstow, Cornwall

This book is printed on acid-free paper

1

'Boss, your father's on the phone, do you want me to put it through to you?' Detective Constable Johnny Dunphy poked his head around the door of Blair's office.

'Tell him I'm in a briefing.'

'The briefing doesn't start for ten minutes.'

'I know that, Johnny, I'm the one giving it.' Blair gave him a withering look. For a promising young detective, he could be remarkably slow on the uptake. 'I just don't want to speak to him.'

'Whatever you say, Boss.' As Johnny disappeared, Blair closed her office door and leant against it for a moment. Would this ever get any easier? Pushing up the sleeve of her suit jacket, the small round scar on her forearm was a reminder that she didn't owe her father anything — least of all her time.

Moving across to the desk, she picked up her notes for the briefing again: a potentially suspicious death in Balloch Pass and what looked like a forged will at the centre of it. Her recent promotion to Detective Inspector had meant a move back to the Highlands, where the small team she headed up was expected to investigate the whole gamut of crimes that occurred in rural Scotland. She'd started her career in child protection, but had moved through to economic fraud, intelligence gathering and finally murder investigations, working for the Met in London, which left her ideally placed to lead a team carrying out a wide range of local investigations. If this suspicious death turned out to be a murder, she'd have to refer it to a regional Major Investigations Team but, at this stage, the Superintendent wanted Blair's team to carry out the ground work.

The last time she'd spoken to her

father, he'd given her the third degree about why she'd left the Met, for what must have been the tenth time. Whatever she said, he couldn't seem to get his head around why she hadn't pursued promotion there, or at least joined one of the Major Investigation Teams in Scotland. He'd never understand that the last thing she wanted was to be like him, so wrapped up in her work that there was no time for anything else. Her new job was demanding, but it was varied, and nowhere near as draining as spending all day, every day, investigating murders, or child protection cases. If she was ever going to put the demons of her own childhood behind her, she had to get away from that. The first big case she'd had with her new team had been an agricultural fraud investigation, involving illegally trafficked workers. It had been traumatic in its own way, but there'd been no crossover into her life, and she liked it that way.

Picking up her mobile, to check for

any updates before she went into the briefing, there were ten missed calls from her father. It was tempting just to block his number, but she wouldn't put it past him to turn up at the station and make a spectacle of them both. He could still find ways of controlling her, even after all this time. An investigation into a suspicious death suddenly seemed like a walk in the park.

* * *

'You and Alasdair don't have to keep inviting me over for dinner, you know.' Noah turned to his friend as the children ran off down the track ahead of them.

'I had an ulterior motive today. How else was I supposed to get all my shopping home?' Evie James laughed, and pointed down at the baby bump that was straining the fabric of her shirt. 'I'm carrying enough excess weight as it is!'

'I couldn't leave you to it when

Alasdair got called out. I'd have picked you up if my car wasn't in the shop.' The handbrake had failed the day before, and it was almost impossible to be a doctor in the Highlands without a car to get out and see patients. It had meant that Noah's colleague at the surgery, Alasdair James, Evie's husband, was having to pick up the slack until it was sorted. So the least he could do was step in and give Evie a hand with the shopping. He'd been at the practice in Balloch Pass for less than a year, but it already felt like home. Alasdair and Evie had been running the surgery between them when he'd first joined, but when she'd found out she was expecting their first baby, they'd both decided to drop their hours to meet the needs of their growing family, and Noah had joined them as a full partner. As well as the fairly imminent arrival of their new baby, they were guardians to Alasdair's godchildren, who'd lost their parents in a car accident a few years before. So they certainly had their hands full. They'd welcomed Noah like an old friend from the outset, and he couldn't imagine ever wanting to leave the small town he'd found completely by chance, when he'd needed a new start of his own. They'd trusted him from the start, too, and no one was constantly checking up on him, or watching his every move. He definitely worked best that way.

Taking a track that ran through a patch of woodland was the quickest way to Alasdair and Evie's house, but it meant passing the Hendry place. Noah had hardly been in Balloch Pass a week when he'd first heard about the Hendry house from a teenage patient who'd visited the surgery complaining of recurring nightmares. The girl had convinced herself that the ridiculous rumours were true. According to her, the house was haunted by widow Hendry, who had died a few years before, and her son was a murderer who'd snatch people walking through the woodland late at night and torture them in his cellar. It was the sort of crazy, unfounded rumour that soon transformed into local legend, especially amongst kids of a certain age; when there was no evidence at all that Colin Hendry had ever done anything but mind his own business. He dressed strangely, and he was a loner who'd lived with his mother his entire life — all of which made him an easy target.

'I don't want to go past the murderer's house.' Bronte, Evie and Alasdair's eight-year-old goddaughter, stuck out her bottom lip. 'He'll put me in his cellar and cook me in the oven!'

'Who on earth told you that?' Evie caught hold of the little girl's hand, stopping her in her tracks.

'Rory did.'

'Is that true?' Evie fixed Bronte's big brother with a look that made Noah want to laugh. His own mother had given him a very similar look whenever he'd pushed his luck as a kid. Rory was in *big* trouble.

'It's true, everyone at school says so. Sid told me he keeps his mother's dead body in the cellar too, propped up in a chair.' Rory's eyes widened as he nodded his head.

'Just because everyone at school says so, it doesn't mean it's true.' Evie still had the same stern look on her face. 'And I don't ever want to hear you talking like that again, or spreading horrible rumours.'

'But it wasn't me that started it.'

'No buts, and no screen time today either.'

'That's not fair! I'm supposed to be playing a game with Sid tonight.'

'Well, when you see him tomorrow, you'll just have to explain to him why you couldn't do it, won't you? And then maybe he'll realise why spreading rumours isn't a nice thing to do, either.'

'But — '

'I've already told you there are no buts. Now hold your sister's hand whilst we walk pass Mr Hendry's house. It's your fault that Bronte's scared of going by, so it's your responsibility to take care of that.' Evie turned towards Noah, as a sulky looking Rory snatched up his sister's hand. 'I'm sorry about that, but I just hate the thought of the kids growing up to be the sort of people who judge someone on what others say about them, rather than finding out the facts for themselves.'

'Don't be silly. It's a lesson in parenting and who knows, one day, in the dark and distant future, I might even need it myself.' Noah smiled, it was something that had crossed his mind since spending so much time with Evie and her family. But with one marriage already behind him, he doubted if it would ever happen. Although if Evie had her way, he'd soon be bringing a plus-one to dinner.

'I've got this friend from when I was working in London, and she's just taken a job as a practice nurse in Loch Lomond. Maybe we could all have dinner together, before this little one arrives and puts pay to my social life for the next ten years or so!'

'I don't know . . . I want to, but I can't help wondering what Katie would think about it.'

'From what you've told me, I think she'd want you to be happy.' Evie squeezed his hand. 'But there's no pressure. I can set it up, if and when you ever feel ready.'

'I'll let you know when I am. Thanks.' Something twisted in Noah's stomach. Whatever he did — or didn't do — Katie was gone, and it was too late to put right the mistakes of the past. The question was, would it ever be time to move on?

* * *

'So what are the grounds for classifying this as a suspicious death then, Boss?' Johnny's voice jolted Blair out of her trance-like state. She hated the fact that the missed calls from her father were having an effect on her, but they were.

'The potential victim was suffering from a few health issues, but none of them were considered life-threatening. And then there's the matter of the will having allegedly been tampered with. The family reported it to the local police immediately after Eileen Dawson's death, and the Chief Inspector wants us to carry out some initial investigations, but it's come direct from the Superintendent.' She didn't add what the Chief Inspector had told her about the Superintendent's long standing friendship with Eileen Dawson's son-in-law. It had to be deemed a potentially suspicious death to be investigated, but it had almost certainly been bumped up the priority list as a result.

'I'm guessing that someone from outside the family stands to benefit from the changes in the will, then?' Bill McGregor, her detective sergeant, had the sort of craggy features that looked like they'd been carved out of Scottish granite. 'Are you sure it's not just some disgruntled family member wanting to get their hands on what they thought they were entitled to?'

'It's our job to find that out. I want you to go and speak to the family, Bill, and you'll need to take Chrissie with you.' Chrissie was another detective constable on the team and a single mother of three teenage boys, with negotiation skills that were second to none as a result. She'd be able to rein in Bill's tendency to go straight for the jugular. Left on his own, he'd probably just ask outright if the family had a vested interest in claiming that the will had been altered. And the direct approach wasn't *always* the best. 'Johnny and I will speak to the pathologist, and then look into the new beneficiaries of the will.'

'You didn't answer my question, though, Boss. *Who* are the new beneficiaries?' Bill was like a dog with a bone, but sometimes he needed reminding that they were launching an investigation, not just searching for evidence to support his gut feeling.

'The local priest and one of Eileen's doctors,' Blair looked down at her notes again, 'a Dr Noah Bradshaw. Apparently she'd hinted she might leave some money to the church, but it was the doctor who was added without Eileen ever mentioning it.'

'And did she have a lot to leave?' Johnny looked up from the notes he was scribbling down.

'Not a lot. She'd signed the house over to her children a few years before, to avoid losing it if she ever had to go into residential care. But there was some jewellery and a few thousand pounds in savings.'

'Hardly worth killing someone over, then.' Bill was shaking his head, his mind clearly made up that this was sour grapes on the family's part. She'd wanted to wait until they were on their own, but she'd have to set him straight now, before he influenced the others.

'I've seen people killed for less than ten pounds, Bill, and sadly a few thousand is more than enough for some people.'

'But surely doctors earn that much in a week?' Bill wasn't giving up.

'We've got no idea at this stage if the doctor is involved or not, and whether we're looking at murder, fraud or just an unexpected death.'

'I can't wait to get stuck into this one.' Johnny shut his notebook and grinned. It might look strange to an outsider, but it was the way born-to-be-coppers were made, and once upon a time she'd been like it too.

2

Meetings with the pathologist had never been a favourite part of Blair's job, but the Procurator Fiscal's office, which was responsible for investigating all suspicious deaths in Scotland, had ordered an immediate autopsy. At least it was a desk-based meeting this time, thank goodness. She'd never quite managed to stop the wobble in her legs, or her voice, no matter how many times she saw a pathologist at work.

'You've seen the reports, I take it?' The pathologist, who was still wearing her scrubs, gestured towards two seats on the opposite side of the desk.

'Yes, thank you.' Blair sat down next to Johnny. 'But it always helps if we can hear it from you, in case there's something between the lines that we're missing.'

'I'm not in the habit of leaving the

outcomes of my reports to guess work, so there shouldn't be any need to '*read between the lines*' as you put it.' Dr Dartford gave her a stony look, the creases around the corners of her mouth suggesting that frowning came naturally. Maybe that was why she chose to spend her days working with the dead, or maybe it was her work that had made her that way. Whatever the reason, it was probably the best fit for her bedside manner, and something about her reminded Blair of her father.

'Fair enough, but we're not in the habit of cutting corners either. So if you could just go through the report, please, that would be really helpful.' Forcing herself to remain polite, in the face of Dr Dartford's bluntness, was starting to make her head pound. 'Was there anything that would flag suspicion?'

'In all likelihood this was death by natural causes, but if I was looking for something unexplained, there is one possibility.' Dr Dartford looked at the notes on her computer screen. 'All signs point to an SCD.'

'SCD?' Johnny was still at the stage of his career where he had to ask those sort of questions.

'Sudden cardiac death. A heart attack if you prefer.'

'But there's another possible cause?' Blair looked at the pathologist levelly. If Dr Dartford thought she could intimidate Blair, she was out of luck: she was an old hand at being patronised.

'The levels of potassium in the blood were significantly raised, which can be the result of either accidental or deliberate poisoning.'

'But you can't be sure?' Blair needed facts, not possibilities.

'In all likelihood, the raised levels of potassium are the result of chemicals being naturally released when the heart muscle was damaged.'

'And that's your best guess?' Blair asked. She could almost sense Johnny's disappointment, his shoulders slumping the longer the pathologist went on. He really wanted this to be something, and he'd made no secret of his ambition to join one of the major investigation teams. But he'd just have to wait for another case to make his mark.

'I don't make guesses.' Dr Dartford's tone was back. 'But, *scientifically*, that's the most plausible outcome. However, given that the SFIU has determined it worthy of further investigation, that's your responsibility.' It had taken Blair a while to get to grips with the fact that sudden and unexplained deaths in Scotland were handled differently from the rest of the UK. The Scottish Fatalities Investigation Unit, overseen by the Procurator Fiscal, took on more or less the same function as the Coroner's Office had when she'd been working at the Met.

'So what could cause this type of potassium poisoning?' Blair wanted as much information as she could get from the pathologist; she didn't want to have to come back.

'Potassium chloride. If the deceased was poisoned by that, it would cause heart spasms and arrhythmia — severely irregular beating of the heart, if you want another lay person's description. Eventually it would stop the heart all together, exactly like a cardiac arrest.'

'And how easy is this potassium chloride to get hold of?' Johnny looked up from his notebook again.

'Almost anything's available if you know the right people. Or the wrong people.' Dr Dartford shook her head. 'Of course the people who'd find it easiest to get hold of, are those in the medical profession. So I'd look at pharmacists or medics first, if I were you.'

'Thank you.' Blair wasn't about to sink to Dr Dartford's level, and tell her she didn't need any advice about doing her own job. First stop would be to interview Dr Bradshaw — that was a given — with or without Dr Dartford's advice.

* * *

'Morning, Doctor.' Aggie Green sat down on the chair in Noah's consulting room with a thud. He checked his screen for the record of her last visit, which had been three weeks before, when she'd come in with a throat infection and he'd prescribed her a week-long course of antibiotics.

'What can I do for you today, Aggie? Has the throat infection completely cleared up?'

'It has, but I'm bone-tired all the time, Doctor. I thought it was the infection at first, but that cleared up over a week ago and I've still got hardly any energy.'

'How are you sleeping?'

'Fine.' Aggie shifted in her seat, looking uncomfortable. 'Well, truth be told, I have had a few restless nights since the post office was closed, but on the whole I get at least six hours a night.'

'You should be aiming for at least six, but more like eight if you can. And is the situation with the post office getting you down?' Persistent tiredness was such a common complaint, and it could be caused by a wide range of reasons, but he wanted to rule out obvious causes, like low mood, first.

'Not so much now that we've decided to fight it.' Aggie suddenly looked animated. 'I'm starting up an appeal campaign, and loads of people have signed up to help. Maybe if a few more of them had signed the petition, and gone on the march through town before it closed, we could have saved the place then.'

'It sounds like you're keeping yourself very busy.'

'It doesn't pay to sit around moping in my experience, Doctor. Taking action is the best way to feel better about something that's getting you down. I just wish I had more energy to do it.'

'Have you given up work now you aren't running the post office?'

Aggie snorted in response to his question. 'Given up work? You are joking, aren't you Doctor? I do home visits for some of the folk who can't get out and about, with bits of shopping and the like. I also do Meals on Wheels three days a week, some housekeeping for Father Douglas, and I've started doing a couple of shifts a week at the petrol station.' Aggie's community spirit put Noah to shame; no wonder she looked so affronted by the suggestion that she'd stopped working. A group of the locals had recently taken over the running of the petrol station, which was the only one for almost twenty miles, and which would have been closed down if they hadn't formed a collective of volunteers to keep it open.

'Do you think you might just be doing too much?' He had to say it, even though he could guess how the suggestion would be received.

'Nonsense! I've always kept busy, it's what suits me best. But, just lately, I don't feel like myself, and sometimes I almost have to drag myself out of bed.' Aggie reached into her handbag and pulled out her mobile phone. 'I've been looking up my symptoms online and I think I might be anaemic.'

'It's a possibility.' He resisted the urge to tell her that Google wasn't fool-proof, but a set of blood tests could rule out her theory, and see whether it might be something else. 'I'm going to give you a form to take to reception, so that you can book in a blood test with the practice nurse. I'm going to ask her to test you for anaemia, thyroid deficiency and vitamin D deficiency. If all of those come back clear, we can look at whether there are any other possibilities. It might just be that you need to make some adjustments to your lifestyle and sleeping patterns.'

'Thank you, Dr Bradshaw. I can't afford to let my energy levels slip, there are too many people relying on me.'

'Remember that sometimes you have to put yourself first, Aggie.'

'Sadly there are all too many folk willing to do that these days.' Aggie pulled a clipboard out of her bag, which was of Mary Poppins' style proportions. 'Talking of which, can I get you to sign my petition to appeal against the post office closure whilst I'm here?'

'Of course.' Noah added his signature, printing the address of the surgery rather than his home address in the box next to it. He couldn't take the chance that Aggie might be one of *those* sorts of patients, who'd turn up at his house if she knew where he lived. Although almost everyone in Balloch Pass seemed to know everyone else's business anyway.

He was just finalising Aggie's notes, after she'd left, when Susie buzzed his phone from reception.

'Sorry, Noah, but there's someone here to see you.' He looked at his watch. Morning surgery was over, but he was running to time, so he didn't mind seeing another patient if it was urgent. He'd never been the sort of doctor who'd been able to prioritise eating his lunch over seeing a patient, and his eating habits were hardly an example for his patients as a result. 'What's the patient's name?'

'Oh, it's not a patient, Dr Bradshaw. There are two police officers here to see you.'

'Right.' The last time two police officers had turned up where he worked, they'd brought the worst possible news to one of his colleagues. But it couldn't be that this time. He was no one's next of kin — not anymore.

'Sorry to barge in on you like this, Doctor, it's good of you to see us. I'm Detective Inspector Blair Hannah, and this is my colleague Detective Constable Johnny Dunphy.' The woman held out her hand.

Whenever Noah heard the word *detective*, he couldn't help picturing a guy in a raincoat, with a weather-beaten face. Years of being subjected to his dad's passion for detective dramas, especially Columbo, had ingrained the image in his psyche. DI Hannah didn't look like she owned a grubby, beige raincoat though, dressed as she was in a fitted grey suit, her long dark hair reaching down past her shoulders.

'Not at all.' Shaking their hands in turn, he still had no idea what they wanted. But there was only really one way to find out. 'Please, sit down. How can I help you?'

'The Procurator Fiscal has opened an investigation into the death of one of your patients. A Mrs Eileen Dawson.'

'Ah, yes. It was difficult to be a hundred percent sure about the cause of death, so the surgery reported it and I understand her family reported it, too. We supplied Mrs Dawson's medical records to the Procurator Fiscal's office.'

'But you weren't able to establish Mrs Dawson's cause of death with confidence?' Detective Hannah had grey eyes that almost perfectly matched her dress, and her gaze never once dropped from his. She might not look like an archetypal TV detective, but she certainly acted like one.

'I was almost certain it was a heart attack, but we hadn't treated Mrs Dawson for a heart condition before, or seen her in the twenty-eight days before her death, so we knew there'd have to be an autopsy. She did have some other ongoing health conditions, though, but it seemed the most likely cause.'

'If you hadn't treated Mrs Dawson in the weeks before her death . . . ' The young detective constable clicked the top of his pen in and out. 'Would you say you knew her well?'

'I saw her more often than the average patient, I suppose. But a lot of the time she relied on repeat prescriptions, unless new symptoms came up.'

'And did you carry out any home visits?' DI Hannah's line of questioning was starting to get uncomfortable. Surely they couldn't suspect him — there was nothing to tie him to Eileen Dawson any more than to his other patients.

'I'd have to double check my notes to be sure, but I think there was only one occasion, when her daughter called me out because she thought Eileen's chest infection might be at risk of turning into pneumonia.'

'Were you and Mrs Dawson alone at any point?' DI Hannah's gaze was unflinching.

'Well, yes, when I examined her. Eileen said she'd rather her daughter stepped out.' Noah ran a finger under the collar of his shirt, which suddenly felt tight. 'Look, I'm sorry, but I don't see what any of this has to do with her death.'

'The thing is, Dr Bradshaw.' DC Dunphy addressed him this time. If they were supposed to be playing '*good cop, bad cop*', Noah had already lost the ability to tell which of them was which. 'It appears from initial investigations that Mrs Dawson had recently changed her will . . . to favour you.'

'There has to be some mistake.' This must be what it felt like to be wrongly accused.

'Her family found a new will after her

death, and you, along with another beneficiary, had been added without Mrs Dawson advising them of the change. The other beneficiary is far less of a shock to the family, because Mrs Dawson had an ongoing relationship with that individual. But you can see why the addition of your name has raised some questions.' DI Hannah paused. 'Especially given the sudden nature of her death.'

'I can, but I don't even know what to say right now. I had no idea. You've got to see this is all a total shock to me too?' Noah was half-expecting to wake up at any minute. This couldn't be real. 'So what happens now, am I under arrest?'

'No, of course not.' The rush of relief that accompanied DI Hannah's words was short-lived. 'But we'll be continuing our investigations, and we'll almost certainly want to speak to you again. So I wouldn't make any plans to leave the area, if I were you, and you should notify us immediately if you do have to leave Balloch Pass for any reason.' DI Hannah handed him her card.

'We'll be in touch.' DC Dunphy looked much more pleased at the prospect than Noah felt. Not that he had anything to worry about, if the police followed the evidence. But there was always a chance that the quiet life he'd found in Balloch Pass — which he'd so desperately needed — was about to come to an abrupt end.

* * *

'So what do you reckon, Boss? Does Dr Bradshaw look like Scotland's answer to Harold Shipman to you?' Johnny's words broke into Blair's thoughts, as they pulled into the car park back at the police station.

'I don't base my analysis on what someone *looks like*, Johnny.' Just as well really, seeing as Dr Bradshaw couldn't have looked less like a potential Harold Shipman-style serial killer. He had warm brown eyes, which had filled with concern at their line of questioning, but that didn't mean he was innocent. She'd seen her own father turn on the charm when it suited him, and when he wasn't playing to the stereotype of the brilliant but aloof consultant. But she'd never forgotten reading Dr Jekyll and Mr Hyde at school, and feeling as if it had been written about him. Some people could hide their true identities, even from themselves. 'Let's see what Bill and Chrissie found out from going through the crematorium records and speaking to the family again.'

'Do you think this could really be part of something bigger, Boss?' Johnny opened the door of the car, that hopeful tone in his voice again. There was a fine line between his enthusiasm and the macabre.

'If Dr Bradshaw is involved, it would be unusual for his actions to be a one-off. Unless he had some significant debt that a one-off murder, with him as the beneficiary, would solve. But in my experience, doctors who do this sort of thing are motivated by more than money. It's more about having the ultimate control, a God complex over whether someone lives or dies.'

'So you've worked on a case like this before?'

'Something similar.' There'd been one case when she was in London, involving a doctor in a residential care home for people with disabilities. But her views about the arrogance some doctors could adopt went way beyond that. Blair wasn't about to share the details of her home life with the young detective, but her father had been all about control, and she'd cowered in her room enough times over the years to believe he'd have been capable of almost anything if she didn't toe the line. 'Hopefully Janey's desk inquiries will show whether Dr Bradshaw had any debts that might have motivated him. All we've got at the moment are a couple of pieces of the jigsaw, and there's no point trying to guess what the whole picture looks like, until we've got the rest. That's a sure fire way of getting caught in the trap of only following one line of inquiry, and that's the worst thing we could do.'

'Absolutely, Boss.' Johnny hung on her every word and Blair had to stop herself laughing at the earnest expression on his face. What would her father make of it? Someone believing she knew everything, instead of being convinced that only he knew what was best for her. She hated her father, or at least the way he treated her the majority of the time. But most of her ambition in the past had come from wanting to prove something to him. And it was why she still hadn't been able to cut him out of her life.

She had a cup of strong black coffee in her hand by the time the team update started ten minutes later. It was bitter, but she liked it that way, the almost unpleasant taste somehow helping to drive unwanted thoughts out of her head. And it was better than having a bottle of vodka in the bottom drawer of her desk, which some of her former colleagues had favoured. Sadly the workaholic, heavy drinking detective wasn't entirely a myth. There were plenty of her former colleagues who'd let off steam in other ways — running marathons, racing motorbikes, or even her first detective sergeant, who worked the amateur stand-up circuit, as a somewhat masochistic form of escapism. But there'd also been enough heavy drinkers amongst them to make her want to avoid going down that route.

'How did your meetings with Chrissie go, Bill?' The two of them exchanged a look, before Bill answered Blair.

'The crematorium staff went through their records with us, and there has been a one hundred and fifty percent increase in cremations, where the death certificates have been signed off by the Balloch Pass surgery, since Dr Bradshaw arrived.'

'But?' It was obvious from the

expression on Bill's face that there was a *'but'* still to come.

'The death certificates were spread amongst all three doctors, and the crematorium manager was adamant that it wouldn't raise any concerns with her as a result. She said in a place the size of Balloch Pass, one or two more deaths than average could skew the data. And, unless all three doctors were in on it, it's nothing more than a few more deaths than average over the past six months.'

'Right.' Blair's shoulders relaxed slightly. It didn't sound as if they had another Harold Shipman on their hands. 'And do you think, from your examination of the records, that any of the deaths warrant further investigation?'

'I think we should speak to the families to see whether there is anything that raises suspicion before we decide whether Eileen Dawson's death, or any of the other deaths in that period, needs to be referred to the Major Investigations Team. We don't even know yet how many of the deaths were unexpected, so the first thing to do is to look into which of them were dealt with by the Procurator Fiscal's office. We should be able to get that information straight away. As you always say, Boss, we've got to pursue every line. For all we know, the crematorium manager could be in on it too!' Bill laughed and inclined his head towards Johnny. He might be taking the mickey out of the newest member of the team, but he had a point. It would be too easy to assume that major crime didn't happen in a place like Balloch Pass.

'Okay, I'd like you and Chrissie to continue to look into that, and speak to the families concerned if you think any of the records warrant further investigation once you've heard back from the Procurator Fiscal's office. We'll have to be careful about how we approach the families, though, we don't want to upset anyone unnecessarily. So I'll want a full briefing before you approach anyone you think you might need to talk to. What about Mrs Dawson's family, how did your follow-up meeting go with them?'

'They're adamant there's no way Eileen would have left money to the doctor without speaking to them first.' Chrissie looked up from her notebook. 'They said she spoke from time to time about wanting to leave some money to the church, but never mentioned having changed her will to that effect. Although, as far as they're concerned, Father Douglas is beyond suspicion.'

'And what are their views on Dr Bradshaw?' The thought that he might be a sociopath capable of putting on such a convincing act was depressing. And if he was, were they putting other patients at risk in the meantime? Making him aware that he was under investigation was all they could do. There was no evidence to tie him to Eileen's death at this stage, and if the surgery didn't want to suspend him in the meantime, the situation was out of her hands. If she was in the habit of going with her gut, she'd say he was innocent, but things were never that easy. As it was, the investigation could go on for weeks, maybe even months.

'They said all three doctors were equally helpful to Eileen when she had to call on them, and, if anything, she had the strongest relationship with Alasdair James, the senior partner.' Chrissie frowned. 'The trouble is, there are already rumours starting to circulate in Balloch Pass about how Noah Bradshaw ended up a widower. Which means it's been easy for the family, and others, to latch on to that. They're upset and they're just looking for someone to blame.'

'What rumours?' Blair held her breath. If there were similar suspicious circumstances around the death of Dr Bradshaw's wife, it could justify a full-blown investigation.

'According to Eileen Dawson's family, he had something to do with his wife's death.'

'It seems unlikely he'd be walking the

streets in that case.' Johnny looked suitably unconvinced.

'Is there anything to suggest that there's any basis to these rumours?' She turned to Chrissie, who shrugged in response.

'Not as far as I can tell, but he's open about having recently been widowed and that his wife had been suffering from a terminal illness. Someone left an anonymous message for Eileen's daughter saying that Dr Bradshaw had helped his wife to die, and that it had obviously given him a taste for it.' Chrissie shook her head. 'It's probably nothing. But for Eileen's relatives, and anyone else in town who fancies themselves as an amateur detective, it seems to have resulted in them putting two and two together and coming up with half a million.'

'We've got to keep an open mind.' Blair was confident the desk investigations would identify whether there was any truth in the gossip. 'Janey, did your research turn up anything about his wife, or his financial situation?'

'There's no significant debt. In fact he owns two properties in London, one that he was living in with his wife until her death last year.'

'And what about the cause of his wife's death? Are there any similarities?'

'She was very ill for a number of years and her death certainly wasn't unexpected. There's nothing in the records to suggest foul play, or even a bit of a helping hand, and it doesn't look like a heart attack either. But her name did come up in a news report about assisted dying, it was something she'd campaigned for, in the months before her death, apparently. That's the trouble with the internet, as much as it's a brilliant tool for me,' Janey pulled a face, 'anyone can look someone up and if they find evidence that fits their theory, then Dr Bradshaw will be marked as guilty long before we even decide if there's enough evidence to refer the case.'

'I don't think we're at the stage yet

where we can make a recommendation either way.' The small team of officers in front of Blair all nodded in agreement. They couldn't drop Eileen Dawson's case until they were a hundred percent sure there was no foul play, from Noah Bradshaw or anyone else.

'So what's next? Are there any other lines of inquiry?' Bill ran a hand through his thinning hair, as Blair nodded in response.

'I'm going to take Johnny to speak to Father Douglas, the priest Eileen left a chunk of her money to, and chat to a few of the locals in Balloch Pass to get a sense of where this gossip might be coming from. That should tell us whether there's someone behind it, who might have their own reasons for putting Dr Bradshaw in the frame. I'm also going to interview the other doctors from the surgery, and you and Chrissie have got the other deaths to follow up. Janey, I'd like you to contact the surgery where Dr Bradshaw worked before, and see if you can speak to any of his late wife's family or friends. I think I can trust you all to use your initiative. I know this is putting you all under a lot more pressure, but we've got to get this right. And not just for Eileen Dawson.'

Janey nodded in response. She didn't say much but, when she did, she had the broadest Scottish accent of the whole team. Unlike Blair, who'd barely ever had a trace of an accent, even before she'd lived in London. Her father had hated her using any of the colloquialisms that might betray her roots, and she'd been told hundreds of times that she didn't sound Scottish. It was just one more aspect of her personality he'd attempted to iron out to suit his own preferences, and she resented the fact it had worked so well.

Blair picked up her coffee cup, as the team filed out of the meeting room to start following up the instructions she'd given them. Calling her father should probably be her priority, before she tried contacting Father Douglas to set up a meeting. But it would have to wait until she felt ready. She was even less sure of when that would be, than she was of who was responsible for Eileen Dawson's death.

3

Despite a reassuring conversation with Alasdair before the start of morning surgery, Noah expected every knock on his consulting room door to be Detective Inspector Blair Hannah. He'd even dreamt about being chased by DC Dunphy, but not being able to run fast enough to get away no matter how hard he tried, and waking up to discover his sheets tangled tightly around his legs. It had been a long time since he'd had such a realistic dream — not since just after Katie had died.

His list for the morning was quieter than normal, too. If it was paranoia to wonder whether it had something to do with the uncertainty surrounding Eileen Dawson's death, then he was in the grip of it.

One upside was that he was able to spend a longer with each of his patients than he usually could. He'd even managed to put a call through to a consultant's secretary at the local hospital, to move Mrs Henry's appointment up. While he'd been on hold, he'd been all too aware of the whispered exchanges between Mrs Henry and her husband, though. And the way she'd looked him up and down, as if appraising whether he really was capable of murdering one of his patients.

His last patient of the morning was Monica Jones, a stoic looking woman in her late forties, wearing a surprisingly short skirt, and with legs that looked as if they were the same thickness from thigh to ankle.

'How can I help you today?' As Noah spoke, she pulled a piece of paper out of her handbag. Thankfully it hadn't been cut from a health column in a newspaper — they were almost as dangerous as the internet.

'I've had an email from my sister in Canada.' Monica was already shaking her head. 'I think it's probably stuff and nonsense, Doctor, but she tells me I might have a hereditary condition she's been diagnosed with, even though I feel absolutely fine.'

'Hopefully it's nothing to worry about, but we ought to look into it.' He silently prayed that it wasn't Huntington's, or anything similar. There was nothing he hated more than not being able to do anything to really help a patient, after a diagnosis like that had been made.

'It's called haemochr . . . it's probably best if you just read the email, Doctor.' Monica pushed the piece of paper towards him.

'Ah, okay, haemochromatosis.' He scanned the email and suppressed a smile at her sister's no-nonsense message '*best get yourself checked out, Mon, before bits start dropping off*'.

'Is it anything to worry about, Dr Bradshaw?'

'Well, your sister is right, it is an inherited disorder, but it's fairly common, especially in people of Celtic descent.' He gave her what he hoped was a reassuring smile. 'But only about a third of people with the condition actually suffer symptoms. Have you had any joint or stomach pain, or increased levels of tiredness?'

'I'm menopausal, Doctor, so I've been tired for about the last three years! I wake up every flipping morning with a sweat outline on the sheets, like the Turin shroud.'

Noah couldn't help laughing. Monica was a real character, and just the sort of patient he liked best — one you could have a laugh with, and who didn't assume that every symptom was the sign of something awful. 'So no unusual pains, or increased levels of tiredness since the symptoms of menopause first started?'

'No, like I say, apart from the night sweats and the resulting insomnia, I'm fit as a flea.'

'Haemochromatosis is caused by a build-up of iron in the body that can result in damage to the organs if left untreated. But if you've got the gene, it certainly doesn't sound like it's causing you any issues. We should get you a blood test to check things out, though, just in case, as the symptoms tend to flare up between the ages of thirty and sixty.'

'What's the outcome if I have got it?' For the first time, Monica looked a bit concerned. 'Only I look after my old da. With Jill in Canada, I'm the only person he's got, and I don't think he'd cope if I wasn't around. He barely ate for the first three weeks after my mother died, and I've seen more flesh on a butcher's pencil.'

'Don't worry too much. If the test is positive, and we get treatment in place before symptoms start showing up, we should be able to manage the condition so that the iron overload doesn't cause any damage.

'Does that mean I'll just have to take a tablet or something?'

'Actually the most effective treatment is phlebotomy.' Noah said, making

Monica furrow her brow in response. 'It just involves taking a small amount of blood, on a regular basis, to reduce the amount of iron in the body.'

'Doesn't sound too bad. My daughter persuaded me to have my armpits waxed last week — she's training to be a beautician — and I've never known pain like it!'

'Hopefully it'll be nothing like as painful. Right, we'll get the blood test done and sent off, and we can take it from there.' He looked at the practice nurse's list on the system. 'Julia should be able to fit you in before she finishes for the day at one o'clock, if you don't mind hanging around for twenty minutes or so?'

'No problem at all, Dr Bradshaw. I don't care what anyone says, there's no way you had anything to do with that business with Eileen Bradshaw, and nearly everyone I've spoken to feels the same.' Monica took the blood test form and he forced a smile. *Nearly* everyone wasn't enough.

'If the results are positive, I'll give you a ring and we can talk a bit more about things then. There's also some really good information and support groups available through the Haemochromatosis Society, so you might want to get in touch with them, even if it's just to find out more because of your sister. I can look it up for you now, if you like?' Searching for the website address, he scribbled it on a piece of paper and passed it to her.

'Thanks again, Dr Bradshaw, keep your chin up.' Monica stood up to leave the consulting room. 'Not to be rude, but I hope I won't see you again too soon, if the test is negative.'

'Absolutely.' Noah just hoped he'd still be around to see Monica, if she needed him when the test results came back. If the rumours about Eileen Bradshaw's death were circulating around Balloch Pass in the way she'd suggested, then — whatever the outcome of the police investigation — it looked like his days at the surgery were numbered.

* * *

The Friday market in Balloch Pass town square was a good place for Blair and Johnny to chat to the locals, to see where the rumours about Dr Bradshaw and his late wife might be coming from. If there was someone fuelling the gossip, they might well have their own reasons for shifting the focus on to the town's newest GP. But if the rumours had some foundation, Blair would have another line of inquiry to follow up.

'Have you managed to get hold of Father Douglas, yet?' Blair pulled into the small car park behind the market square, thankful to find a parking place at all on market day.

'I've left three messages now, but he never answers his phone. You'd think a priest would need to be on call all the time, wouldn't you? In case he needs to perform the last rites or something.' Johnny laughed. The lack of dark circles under his eyes, or any sign that he might be tired, irritated Blair. He had a good ten years on her, but there was no excuse to look so fresh-faced, especially when her fail-safe concealer had just sunk into the black shadows under her eyes, without making the slightest impact.

'We've got to meet up with the community police constable in five minutes, but maybe we should knock at Father Douglas' place afterwards and see if he's there?' She took the keys out of the ignition. 'He might even be avoiding our phone calls on purpose.'

'You don't seriously think a priest could have anything to do with this, do you?' Johnny already seemed to have made his mind up that Dr Bradshaw was the chief suspect. But experience had taught her that there was no such thing as being above the law, whatever you did for a living.

'We've got to talk to him. I know the family are convinced he had no part in this, but how will it look if we only pursue inquiries about one of the beneficiaries of the will?'

'And this police constable, do you think she's going to know something useful?'

'She's got local knowledge and it gives us a uniformed presence. If someone has something to say about the case to the police, then they're more like to do it if Vicky is with us.' Opening the door of the car, Blair waited for Johnny to follow suit. The fact that he thought involving the community police constable was a waste of time was just another reminder that he still had a lot to learn. Everyone had a role to play, and having Vicky with them might just make all the difference.

They didn't speak as they crossed the car park, with Johnny loping along behind like a moody teenager. Vicky was waiting for them on the edge of the market square, and his demeanour changed as soon as he set eyes on her. She was young, blonde and petite and, from the conversations Blair had overheard Johnny having with the other lads at the station, right up his street.

'Detective Inspector Hannah?' PC Vicky Nesbitt smiled in greeting. 'I've read a lot about the work you've done, and it's an honour to be working with you on this case.'

'We'll really value your input. And, with a build-up like that, I just hope we don't disappoint you!' Blair turned to Johnny, who seemed to have been struck dumb. 'This is DC Dunphy, but I'm almost certain he won't mind if you call him Johnny.'

'Absolutely, if I can call you Vicky?' Johnny grinned, and Blair made a bet with herself. If the two of them hadn't exchanged mobile numbers by the end of the day, she might as well give up being a detective, because she'd have totally lost her ability to read people.

They spent the next ten minutes or so discussing the case, and finding out what, if anything, Vicky already knew about the rumours relating to Noah Bradshaw and his wife.

'Isn't that the man himself, over there?' Johnny pointed between two of the stalls, as they made their way around the edge of the market. He was right; Noah Bradshaw was standing by the greengrocer's, a baseball cap pulled down over his eyes. But he was unmistakeable all the same.

'I suppose even murder suspects have to buy potatoes!' Johnny laughed far too hard at Vicky's joke, and Noah's head shot up — making direct eye contact with Blair.

'Are you following me?' Noah said, as they walked towards one another.

'Should I be?'

'Not unless you're particularly interested in the current market price of sweet potatoes or you've got time to kill, like me, because someone's stopping you from doing your job.' His mouth was set in a firm line, and she knew what he was going to say, before he even said it. 'Because of your investigation, there are patients who won't see me, so my first three appointment slots this afternoon are empty. Don't get me wrong, I'm all for getting an extended lunch break, but it just puts more pressure on my colleagues. And if it goes on much longer, I can't see a way of me being able to carry on here.'

'These things take time, and it hasn't been that long at all yet.' She put her hands on her hips, a muscle pulsing in his cheek as she spoke. This wasn't helping.

'And are you investigating anyone else?'

'We're following several lines of inquiry.'

'And so you should be.' A woman's voice cut into their conversation, and Blair turned to see two women, who looked to be in their late sixties, standing between Johnny and Vicky. 'I was just saying to this wee lassie that you've got this all wrong. The doc here is brilliant, he's been out to see me a couple of times, out-of-hours, when my fibromyalgia got the better of me. Nothing is ever too much bother for him, and he got to the bottom of your tiredness too, didn't he, Aggie?'

'Aye, he did indeed, Janet.'

'We need a bit more than a character reference in a case like this, unfortunately.' Johnny turned to the first woman and smiled, but she wagged a finger at him in response.

'Well, I'm telling you that you're barking up the wrong tree. You want to be looking at that Colin Hendry. Ever since his mother died, he was always round at Eileen's place, supposedly playing cards. But I reckon if anyone is weird enough to do something like this, it's him. Creepy wee fella, and all the rumours about him not reporting his mother's death straight away seem to have a lot more basis than your crackpot theories.'

'I appreciate your support, Janet.' Noah laid a hand on the woman's arm. 'But it's just as bad to suggest that Colin might have something to do with this. Just because he lives his life a bit differently to the rest of us, that doesn't make him a killer. And I don't like seeing anyone victimised in the way he is.'

'All I'm saying, Doc, is that these detectives need to open their eyes and stop listening to idle gossip about what happened before you left London.' The irony of Janet's words seemed completely lost on her. Idle gossip was obviously okay when it suited her.

'If anyone has the guts to ask me outright, then they'll get a straight answer. My wife died of a terminal illness, and in her last weeks she decided not to have any more treatment. I supported her decision. And if that makes me a killer in some people's eyes, then I'd much rather live with that than the knowledge I let her down when she needed my support.' Even under the peak of his cap, Noah's eyes were clearly blazing. Blair recognised that look — the knowledge that the right thing had been done, even if no one else saw it like that.

'You've no need to explain yourself to us, has he Aggie?' Janet looked at her friend for agreement, before gesturing towards the three officers. 'I just wanted this lot to know that listening to all the nonsense about you is slowing them down from finding the real killer. If there even is one. Eileen Dawson was far too fond of an afternoon tipple during those card games, in my opinion. I told her more than once that no good would come of it. Colin Hendry might not have killed her, but those bottles of stout he brought her in most days are as likely to be to blame as anything. Maybe she had one too many and decided to change the will, but forgot to tell those money-grasping children of hers. That's just as likely as anything else.'

'Thank you for being so candid.' Blair handed Janet her card. 'We'll certainly consider whether we need to look into Mr Hendry's relationship with Mrs Dawson, but if you think of anything else that might be useful in the meantime, please feel free to give me a call.'

Whether they'd found another potential suspect in Colin Hendry remained to be seen, but the conversation with Janet and Aggie had been useful anyway. Noah's reaction to talking about his late wife had revealed a lot, too. And, unless her instinct at reading people *was* totally off, he'd had nothing to do with her death.

As the two older women walked away from them, one of the stallholders approached Vicky to complain about the level of theft in the market, and to ask what she was doing about it. Johnny was glued to the young police constable's side, interjecting in a discussion that had absolutely nothing to do with him. But it suited Blair — Noah was far more likely to open up to her without Johnny in the middle of it.

'You've got quite the fan club there, so there are obviously still plenty of patients in Balloch Pass more than happy for you to be their doctor.'

'I don't want any of my patients having to step in and defend me from something I haven't done, especially when someone like Colin Hendry is being put in the frame instead.' Noah's eyes met hers. 'You don't want to listen to anything they said about him, by the way. He's just a lonely man, who's really misunderstood. He was probably as affected as anyone by Eileen's death.'

'Even if it takes the heat off you?'

'I'm not interested in anything but the truth and I'm hoping you feel the same, given I'm relying on you to clear my name.'

'Of course we do. That's our only focus.' Blair glanced in Johnny's direction, not entirely sure she should be making that promise for both of them. The disgruntled stallholder had moved on, and Johnny appeared to be exchanging numbers with the community police constable, whose help he had been so willing to dismiss before he saw her. Blair might have been right, but it gave her no satisfaction.

'Janet and Aggie meant well, but they're both inclined to buy into the gossip. And with Aggie being Father Douglas' housekeeper, she hears more than her fair share of it, but that doesn't mean any of it's true. I'd stake everything I own that Colin had nothing to do with Eileen's death.'

'Should it worry me that you seem so certain?' Blair said, making him sigh in response. 'Look, I'm sorry, but I had to ask. Thanks for the heads up, but I need to speak to Aggie again, regardless. We've been trying to get hold of Father Douglas for a couple of days now without success, so maybe Aggie can shed some light on that too.'

'He's at a retreat on the Isle of Skye, but he'll be back late tonight. Aggie mentioned it when she popped into the surgery this morning.'

'Is there nothing you don't know about what's going on in Balloch Pass?'

'I don't know if anyone was involved in Eileen's death, or why on earth her will was changed to mention me.' Noah's dark eyes clouded. 'I just wish I did.'

Watching him walk away, Blair wished she knew for sure too. Every time she met Noah, she was more and more convinced he'd had nothing to do with Eileen's death. But she didn't want to hand it over to the Major Investigation Team until she was certain of that. There was one thing she already knew, though — she didn't *want* it to be Noah.

* * *

'Yay, it's Noah!' Bronte opened the door to Evie and Alasdair's house, with such a big smile on her face that Noah's mood lifted momentarily. Evie appeared in the corridor behind the little girl seconds later.

'Are you going to let him in then, darling?' She raised her eyebrows, as Bronte grabbed Noah by the hand and dragged him along the corridor.

'Can I do the drinks, Mammy?' The words tripped off Bronte's tongue, as if she'd been saying them all her life. But

Alasdair had confided in Noah that the 'Mammy and Daddy' labels were a recent development. When Alasdair and Evie had become the children's guardians after their parents' death, they'd been 'Auntie and Uncle' for the first year. With a new baby on the way, Bronte had asked them if she could call them Mammy and Daddy, and it had been an emotional time from what Alasdair had said. He'd even asked Noah's advice, despite the fact that he knew next to nothing about parenting, and even less about raising someone else's child. Alasdair had wanted his opinion on whether he was betraying his friends, by letting Bronte call them Mammy and Daddy. Especially as her brother, Rory, was more than happy to stick to Auntie and Uncle. Noah doubted his advice had been of any use, but he could only say what he thought — if it made Bronte happy, then it had to be the right thing to do.

'Of course you can do the drinks, darling. Go through to the kitchen and ask Unc . . . Daddy to give you a hand.' She turned to Noah, as Bronte skipped ahead of them. 'How are you holding up?'

'Fine, apart from being hounded by Scotland's finest, and having more cancelled appointments in the last week than I've had in the rest of the time I've been here.' Noah shook his head; he didn't want to spend the whole night talking about it. 'More to the point, how are you?'

'Put it this way, if I turned sideways my stomach would pin you against the wall, and I've now got a bottle a day habit — of Gaviscon.'

'It'll all be worth it in the end.' He followed her through to the kitchen, where Alasdair was helping Bronte get some drinks out of the fridge. Rory was in charge of stirring whatever it was that was cooking, and he was wearing a chef's hat that was at least three sizes too big for him, emblazoned with the words *King of the Grill*.

'Evening Noah, what will it be?

Mineral water, orange juice, or maybe something a bit stronger?' Alasdair handed Bronte a bottle of sparking water and she cradled it like a baby.

'Water's fine for now, thanks.' If he started drinking this early, he might not even make morning surgery — regardless of whether there were any patients who actually wanted to see him. He was going to be raising a glass or two to Katie later, eighteen months to the day since his wife had died, but that was something else he wasn't intending to share. Just for an hour or two, he wanted to forget that he was under investigation for a possible murder, and that he was a widower who didn't deserve the level of sympathy that title always evoked.

After a dinner with the whole James family, and some tough negotiation from Bronte, they had to play two games of Ludo before she and Rory would go to bed. When Evie took them upstairs, Alasdair uncorked a bottle of red wine and poured Noah a large glass, without even asking if he wanted it.

'I thought you could use this. Susie says it's been a tough few days for you at the surgery.' Alasdair handed him a glass. Their receptionist had been nothing but supportive, but she must have been under pressure from patients demanding appointments with anyone but Noah. If this didn't get resolved soon, he really might have to resign. But since he wasn't allowed to leave Balloch Pass without telling DI Hannah, he'd end up having to get a job in the Co-op at this rate. Although, given his current reputation, there were no guarantees he could even do that.

'I just feel like I'm letting you and Evie down.' The one person he wanted to speak to about all of it was Katie. She'd always given the best advice, and he missed that so much.

'Don't be daft. None of this is your fault. We haven't had a moment's doubt about that.'

'How can you be so sure?' He was

doing it again, challenging someone who said they believed him — just like he'd done with DI Hannah. What the hell was wrong with him?

'Because I've seen you with patients, and there are just some things you have total faith in.' Alasdair raised his glass. 'I had the pleasure of meeting DI Hannah earlier and I've got faith in her, too. If anyone can get to the bottom of this, she will.'

'And what if more and more patients refuse to see me in the meantime? The point of me joining the practice was to take the pressure off you and Evie, not add to it.'

'It'll be over by this time next week; DI Hannah said she was hopeful they'd be able to make a decision by then about whether to refer the case on. They'll realise there's no case to answer, and my bet is that Eileen changed her will because you did more to support her than her own family. Unfortunately, it happens a lot.' Alasdair took another drink.

'I didn't do any more for Eileen than you or Evie. And what if they decide the case does need to be referred on?' He had no idea how the criminal investigation system worked in Scotland, he just knew a referral of the case meant it was serious.

'We'll worry about that if it comes to it.' Alasdair looked at him levelly. 'Which it won't. How are you otherwise? It's coming up to a year and a half since you lost Katie, isn't it?'

'You've got a good memory, but I'm okay, honestly.' The mouthful of wine Noah took warmed the back of his throat. He wasn't about to tell Alasdair that it was exactly eighteen months since Katie had died. Alasdair was a good friend to remember as much detail as he did from the conversations they'd had. And it was all the more reason why Noah didn't want to let him down, or say too much more about what had really happened with Katie. Not a lot of people would understand why he'd done what he had, and he'd questioned it himself hundreds of times in the months since her death.

'It must be such a tough time for you. Why don't you take some time out this weekend and go and stay in the cabin?' Alasdair had mentioned the cabin he and Evie owned in the forest, at Coille Water, on the edge of Balloch Pass, and Noah had to admit it sounded idyllic. But the last thing he wanted was for Alasdair to lend him the place under false pretences.

'That might look even more suspicious. A cabin in the woods is just where they'd expect a suspected murderer to hang out!' Making light of it was the only way to get through. Of all the things he thought he might be accused of as a result of moving to Scotland so soon after his wife's death, murdering one of his patients wasn't one of them.

'Well, the offer's there if you want it.' Alasdair topped up their glasses as Evie came back to join them at the table. Neither of them pressed him to talk more about Eileen Dawson, or his wife's death, and he managed to enjoy the rest of the evening, almost pushing it to the back of his mind as a result. They were good people, and one thing he wouldn't do was drag them down with him, whatever the cost.

4

The door knocker at the chapel house was so shiny that Blair could see her reflection in it, and the shape distorted her face, like something from a house of mirrors at a fun fair. At least she hoped it was down to the contours of the door knocker, and not the fact she'd hardly slept for the past week.

'Can I help you?' Blair immediately recognised the woman who answered the door to Father Douglas' house. It was Aggie Green, one of the women from the market place who'd defended Noah so vehemently, and who he'd said was the priest's part-time housekeeper. She was wearing a wrap-around apron, and an expression that suggested their visit wasn't altogether welcome.

'We've got an appointment to see Father Douglas; DI Hannah and DC Dunphy.' The older woman made no move to step aside.

'I'll need to see your ID.'

'Of course.' Blair took out her warrant card and gestured to Johnny to do the same. Aggie Green must have recognised her from the market place too, but she seemed determined not to make this easy. Clearly she was as protective of Father Douglas as she was of Noah. There might be a lot of gossip in a small town like Balloch Pass, but they could close ranks in support of one of their own, and it was almost impossible to get anyone to talk when that happened. Blair had seen it before, when she'd first moved back, and after all those years in the Met it had been quite a culture shock. Not that there weren't people in the city willing to protect one of their own at all costs. But for some of them, it was more likely to be tied to gang affiliation than a sense of community, and speaking out could carry the ultimate price.

'I suppose you'd better come in, but Father Douglas needs his rest these days so I don't want you keeping him long.' Aggie finally stepped to one side. 'You can wait in the drawing room and I'll go and get him.'

'Thank you.' Blair wasn't about to argue with the woman. Aggie was the sort of person who would know exactly what was going on in Balloch Pass and, if she could win her trust somehow, she might even have some useful information.

'These sort of places give me the creeps.' Johnny ran a hand along a shelf lined with artificial flowers in crystal vases, and a collection of porcelain and crystal bells. 'There's not a speck of dust on these shelves, even though he's got more old tatt than my gran.'

'I don't think Aggie Green is the sort of person to let a speck of dust get past her.'

'She certainly isn't!' Father Douglas shuffled into the room, looking about as far removed from a murder suspect as it was possible to do. Not only was he unsteady on his feet, but he was smiling in such a welcoming way — especially after the frosty reception Aggie had given them — that it was almost impossible to believe he could be hiding a dark side. *Almost*.

People could put on an act and some of them were scarily good at it. Blair tugged at the sleeve of her dress, suddenly conscious that the scar on her forearm might be showing. Priests were good at reading people, too. And the last thing she wanted was Father Douglas getting an insight into *her* dark side, whilst she was still trying to discover his.

'Aggie has already warned us that we mustn't keep you too long.' Blair returned his smile. 'Thank you for agreeing to see us, Father Douglas. I'm DI Hannah — we spoke on the phone — and this is my colleague, DC Dunphy.'

'Good to meet you both and don't worry about me, I'm more robust that I look.' Father Douglas laughed, as he shook their hands in turn. 'But then I'd have to be really, wouldn't I? Or a rough wind would blow me into the nearest loch! Please take a seat. I've asked Aggie to bring us some tea, and don't worry, you can keep me as long as you need me. I might even be able to persuade her to bring us some cake, if she's feeling charitable.'

'I'm not sure we're on her list of favourite people.' Blair sat opposite the chair Father Douglas had taken, with Johnny sitting to the right.

'She's a big fan of Dr Bradshaw — as am I — so any suggestion that he might be involved in something sinister was bound to meet with one of her famous thin-lipped responses.' Father Douglas laughed again. 'And then, of course, there's the fact that you've asked to speak with me.'

'We're just making sure we follow up all lines of inquiry, before a decision is made about whether there's actually a case to look into, let alone who might be responsible for Mrs Dawson's death.' Blair didn't miss the slight inclination of Father Douglas' head. Was he surprised that there might not even be a murder investigation? Maybe he knew more than he was saying, even if it was only about Mrs Dawson's state of mind just before her death. After all, her family weren't that surprised that she'd left a portion of her estate to him, because Eileen had gone to confession on a weekly basis, right up until her mobility had been impaired, and then Father Douglas had started to visit her instead.

'Of course you've got to be thorough, and I understand that, but Aggie . . . She's of the old school, where doctors and priests are beyond reproach. We both know that's not true, don't we?' There was definite twinkle in Father Douglas' eyes, and he didn't seem remotely concerned that they were there to decide whether they could eliminate him from their inquiries. But why would he be, if he had nothing to hide?

'And you say you're a big fan of Dr

Bradshaw, too?' Johnny asked the question, his notebook at the ready.

'I think he's been an asset to the town, and he's clearly a doctor who's willing to go the extra mile. But that's not what you're really asking is it?' He looked at Johnny.

''I, er . . . '

'What you're asking, is whether I think Dr Bradshaw had anything to do with Eileen Dawson's death? Am I right?' All Johnny could do was nod in response. 'In that case the answer is no.'

'How can you be so sure?' Blair would finish the question, even if Johnny couldn't

'Only God knows for *sure*.' Father Douglas looked up as he spoke. 'But I'm an old man, and I've met lots of good people in my time and lots of bad people — I think I've learned over the years how to tell the difference.'

'And what about Mrs Dawson, did she have any enemies as far as you know, or problems that might have caused her to take her own life?' Blair caught the look that crossed his face. It was almost as if the shutters had come down.

'She wouldn't have done that. Eileen was a good Catholic woman, and anything she shared with me in confession is between Eileen and God now.'

'I wasn't asking you to break a confidence. We're just trying to understand what happened and whether we need to turn this suspicious death into a murder inquiry.' Blair paused for a moment; what she was going to ask next would probably make Father Douglas close down altogether, but she had to do it. 'And what about your relationship with Mrs Dawson? Were you surprised about her intention to leave you some money?'

'She certainly hadn't ever mentioned it, although it's happened before. The fact is, anything that's left to me personally is given to the church. You can look back at my records, if you like, but there would be nothing for me to personally gain from inheriting the money. So, if you're looking for a motive, then I'm afraid you're out of luck.'

'And what about Mrs Dawson having enemies?' Johnny's desire to see a murder investigation opened wasn't showing any signs of easing off. It was just another step on the ladder for him, but he was going to have to develop a bit more empathy if he was going to really learn to understand people.

'She mostly kept herself to herself, except for her friendship with Colin Hendry, and seeing her own family. I can't imagine her having the opportunity to make enemies, let alone the sort who'd want to murder her.'

'Do you think Colin Hendry could have had something to do with her death?' Johnny scribbled something down in his notebook as he spoke, but Father Douglas was already shaking his head.

'Anything's possible, but Eileen was his mother's best friend, and after

Maureen Hendry died, Eileen all but took her place in Colin's life.' Father Douglas looked up again, as Aggie pushed open the door of the drawing room.

'Your tea.' Setting the tray down on the table, she lifted a clipboard off the top and handed it to Blair. 'And if you sign this, I might even bring you a wee bit of cake.'

'What is it?'

'It'll be Aggie's petition to get the post office reopened.' Father Douglas smiled. 'She never misses an opportunity to collect another signature.'

'Aye, that's right, but it's for a good cause. That place was almost as much of a lifeline for some folks as the church.'

'I'll not argue with you there.' Father Douglas poured out some tea, as Blair signed the petition and passed it on to Johnny. There was no harm in getting Aggie on side.

'And I'm a woman of my word; I'll get you all some cake. I've got chocolate cake, or carrot cake with a cream cheese and walnut topping.'

'Either is fine for me.' Blair's stomach grumbled at the thought. If her dad knew she was living on caffeine and quick hits of sugar, like she had for the past few days, he'd have been horrified — which did very little to put her off.

"I'd better steer clear.' Johnny handed the petition back to Aggie.

'I suppose you're one of these young people who'd rather I whipped you up a smoothie full of green stuff?' Aggie seemed to take the refusal of cake as a personal insult.

'No, I'd love some, but I have a nut allergy and it's just not worth the risk.'

'You've never tasted *my* baking.' Aggie put the clipboard under her arm, and it was impossible to tell whether she was joking — her expression deadpan as she left the room.

'She's quite a character, Aggie, isn't she?' Blair took the cup of tea that Father Douglas passed her.

'She's a one-off!' The priest rolled his

eyes. 'But she does a lot for me and the community as a whole; she's still offering some of the services she ran out of the post office, even though it's closed. There are not many people like that around.'

'Sadly, you're right.' Blair fought the urge to sigh. The investigation was getting nowhere fast, and speaking to Father Douglas hadn't got them any closer to finding out whether there was someone who wanted Eileen Dawson dead. But it still didn't put Noah Bradshaw completely in the clear, either. Colin Hendry's name had come up again, though. And, as harmless as Father Douglas seemed to think he was, it was time to follow that up. Colin hadn't been left any money, and there was no clear motive for him wanting Eileen dead, but Blair knew better than anyone that people didn't always behave in ways that made sense.

* * *

'Jesus, this place looks like something out of the Addams family.' Johnny shifted from foot to foot as they stood outside the door of Colin Hendry's house. It was down a long track and half-hidden by an overgrown patch of woodland. No wonder the rumours were rife in town about him — his house was like a caricature of a serial killer's lair, with filthy windows and even a lump of rope hanging, like a makeshift noose, from a branch on the tree nearest to the house.

'It doesn't mean he's done anything wrong. Let's not jump to conclusions.' Arresting Colin would have been a neat close to the investigation, and solving it before they passed the case to a Major Investigation Team was certainly appealing. But Blair couldn't get Noah's words out of her head. Colin was too easy a target to pin this on, and maybe someone wanted it that way. Noah might even be double bluffing, defending Colin so it wouldn't look like he was the one trying to pin Eileen's murder on him. Even knowing whether they were definitely dealing with a murder would have felt like massive progress.

'Can I help you?' The man peering through a crack in the door had pale skin and thinning hair.

'Colin Hendry?' Blair held up her warrant card. 'Detective Inspector Hannah, and Detective Constable Dunphy. Can we come in and have a word?'

'The place is a bit of a m-m-mess.' Colin had a stutter and one of his eyes twitched when he spoke, but he pulled back the door to let them in. 'Go through the first door on the left, and we can sit in there.'

The hallway had piles of old newspapers with boxes stacked on top of them, so they had to turn sideways as Colin led the way into the room. He gestured towards one of the sofas, which was patterned but so dirty it was hard to make out exactly what the pattern was supposed to be. Perching on the edge of the sofa, Blair sent up a cloud of dust as she sat down, but Colin stayed standing. The shelves and sideboard behind him were stacked high with things too, giving the room the appearance of an old junk shop in desperate need of sorting out.

'W-w-why do you want to speak to me?'

'It's about Eileen Dawson's death.' Johnny leapt in with the answer, and the twitching of Colin's eye doubled its pace. A softly-softly approach to the subject would probably have worked better, but it was too late now.

'She was my f-f-friend, I didn't do anything to her.'

'No one is saying that you did, and we don't even know for sure whether what happened to Eileen was suspicious at all.' Blair adopted a deliberately gentle tone. 'You were obviously close to Eileen, and spent a lot of time with her. Did she ever mention her intention to leave money to Dr Bradshaw or Father Douglas?'

'We d-d-didn't talk about that sort of

stuff, but they're b-b-both good men.' Colin was sticking to the party line, and no one seemed to have a bad word to say about either of Eileen Dawson's beneficiaries. Maybe that was why she'd left them the money and it really was as simple as that.

'What about you and Eileen, did the two of you ever fall out?' Johnny flipped open his notebook, and Colin started to shake his head rapidly.

'No! She was like my second mother and I m-m-miss her.' Colin's breathing had changed, and within seconds it had started to come in short, raspy breaths, his earlier pallor changing to a deep red.

'Sit down and relax, just breathe.' Blair got to her feet and helped Colin to sit down. 'Just concentrate on your breathing, and put your head between your knees if it helps.' She had no idea what she was doing and Johnny was running his hands through his hair — hardly the calming influence she needed. 'Johnny, I think we might need an ambulance, but if one of the doctors at the surgery is free, that would be great. That way we'll know we're doing the right thing until it arrives. If you head over there and call for an ambulance on the way, I'll stay here with Colin.'

'Yes, Boss.' Johnny didn't need asking twice, the front door slamming behind him just seconds later.

'Take a deep breath in through your nose, and hold it for a count of three seconds if you can, then slowly release the breath through your mouth.' Blair needed to take her own advice. Her hands were shaking and Colin's eyes were glassy. Unless he was giving an Oscar-winning performance, Colin Hendry was having a massive panic attack, or maybe something even worse, at the mere suggestion he might have fallen out with Eileen Bradshaw. Every instinct Blair had was screaming that there was no way this man was capable of murder. But whatever the truth, one thing was absolutely certain

— she didn't want him to die on her watch.

* * *

'So what do you reckon is causing the pain, Doc?' Danny McGuire pulled on his sock as he asked the question.

'Given what you've told me, and the sites of pain, I think the most likely cause is Plantar Fasciitis.'

'Is it serious, Doc?'

'No, it's caused when you get tiny tears in the fibrous tissue that runs between your heel and your toes. The tears cause inflammation and that's the pain you've been experiencing.' Noah washed his hands. 'With the hours you spend on your feet, it's likely that's put more of a strain on the tissues.'

'Will I need an operation?' Danny McGuire owned the butcher's in Balloch Pass and he was a big built man, but he widened his eyes at the possibility of a surgeon taking the knife to him for a change.

'No, not unless it turns out to be something else, or if you develop heel spurs that we can't get rid of. But our starting point for treatment will be rest, some gentle exercises, applying ice to the area and, if you'd like to try it, some anti-inflammatory medication to take the swelling down.'

'Much as I'd like a rest, Doc, I can't afford to have someone else in the shop six days a week, so I'll be on my feet most of the time whether I like it or not.'

'In that case, we can try the medication, and if that doesn't work there's always the option of steroid injections in the heel.' Noah couldn't help laughing at the expression on Danny's face.

'A needle? Straight into my foot?'

'Yes, but like I say, that's an option we can consider if the other things don't work. There are also some useful aids you can get, including shock-absorbing heel cups.'

'Aye, Doc, I think I'd rather try those

out for a while before we talk about injections.'

'I'll give you a prescription for the anti-inflammatories, and we've got some leaflets out in reception about heel pain and the exercises you can do relieve it, as well as some of the aids available.' Noah handed Danny the prescription. 'I'll walk you out, I need to speak to Susie about something anyway, and I can show you where to find the information you need.'

'You might be the talk of the town, Doc, but you're still the best doctor I've ever had.' Danny grinned, his mouth almost hidden in the depths of his bushy ginger beard, and Noah nodded in response. Would the back-handed comments go away, once they discovered what had really happened to Eileen Bradshaw? There was always a risk that the investigation would uncover things that would change people's opinions about Noah forever, even when he was completely cleared of any involvement in her death. But there was still that first hurdle to clear for now, and he'd worry about the rest when he had to. He hoped his faith in Blair Hannah wasn't misplaced.

'We need a doctor, quickly!' Detective Constable Dunphy flew through the doors of the surgery and nearly knocked the rack of leaflets, beside which Noah and Danny were standing, off the wall. 'It's Colin Hendry, he's having some sort of attack and he can't breathe. I've called an ambulance but the colour he was when I left him . . . I'm not sure he's going to make it!'

'Is he there on his own?' Noah caught hold of DC Dunphy's arm to slow him down.

'No, Blair is there with him trying to calm him down, but I don't think it's working. Can you come over?'

'Of course.' Noah turned to the reception desk. 'Can you speak to Alasdair when he finishes with his patient, and let him know where I am? Depending on what happens, he might have to see my last couple of patients before lunch.

I might not be able to leave Colin until the ambulance arrives.'

'Don't worry, we'll sort it out.' Susie got to her feet. 'Is there anything you need me to get for you?'

'I'll grab my bag, if you could get me the oxygen tank and mask, just in case?' Noah was already heading back to his consulting room; there was no time to waste.

* * *

'Oh thank goodness!' Blair answered the door when they got to Colin's place. 'He's in the lounge and I've tried to count his breathing in and out, but he just doesn't seem able to get it back under control.

'Can you see if you can find me a book or a magazine?' Noah turned towards DC Dunphy, who was looking at him as though he'd completely lost it. 'Trust me, if this is a panic attack, it could help him regulate his breathing again.'

'Colin, Dr Bradshaw is here.' Blair spoke as Noah followed her into the front room. Colin's breathing was so rapid he didn't even acknowledge their arrival.

'It's Noah.' He knelt down beside him. 'Have you ever had an attack like this before?'

'N-n-nothing like this.' Colin struggled to get the words out.

'Any chest pains?' Colin managed to shake his head in response, as Noah took his pulse. It was very rapid. 'Have you got pain anywhere else?'

'Tingling and cramping.' Even answering the questions seemed to be helping Colin to slow his breathing and when DC Dunphy returned with a copy of the local paper, Noah passed it to his patient.

'I want you to read one of the articles on the front page.' This was their best chance of helping Colin.

'Seventy nine households were c-c-caught up in the recent Highland floods, which affected at least five p-p-properties in Balloch Pass.'

'That's good, now carry on. I'm just going to take your blood pressure, okay?' Noah pushed Colin's sleeve up and tightened the blood pressure cuff over his upper arm. His BP was raised, but not by as much as it could have been, and his colour was already starting to look a bit more normal. If reading from the paper hadn't helped, Noah's back up plan would have been to give Colin the oxygen mask without attaching it to the tank. Giving Colin oxygen wouldn't have hurt him, but it would have taken longer for his breathing to get back to normal. Thankfully, there was no need to do that now.

'Shall I ring and cancel the ambulance?' Blair's voice broke into his thoughts. He'd almost forgotten she was there, and that she still saw him as a potential suspect.

'I think he should probably go in and get checked over, just to be on the safe side. From what you've managed to tell us, you haven't had one of these attacks before, have you, Colin?'

The older man shook his head. 'I thought I was dying.'

'It really feels that way when you're in the middle of a panic attack, but I promise you that nothing like that is happening. Just keep concentrating on your breathing.'

'Thank you.' Blair put a hand on his arm and he returned her smile. If he had to entrust anyone with clearing his name, he was glad it was her.

* * *

Slamming the ambulance doors, the paramedic walked around to the front of the vehicle and within seconds they were pulling away. Noah was going with Colin to the hospital, even though his breathing was almost back to normal by the time the paramedics had turned up. As he'd never had a panic attack before, the crew had decided to err on the side of caution and take him into the nearest

A&E for a check-up. No easy feat from a remote Highlands town, although getting him out of the hallway of his house in their carry chair had been a challenge in itself.

'Do you think his reaction suggests anything about his possible involvement in Eileen's death?' Johnny looked more like his old self, but she'd seen the look of panic on his face during Colin's attack, no matter how casual he tried to be about it now.

'I think it says more about how much pressure he's been under, and how much he'd probably come to rely on Eileen Dawson after his mother's death. I just can't see him doing anything to risk losing a second mother figure.'

'He's obviously got a close allegiance with Dr Bradshaw. It was like someone had flicked a switch when he turned up. I've never seen such a quick change.' Johnny narrowed his eyes.

'And what? That means they're in it together, does it?'

'I'm not jumping to any conclusions,

Boss. Like you said.' Johnny dropped a wink. 'But did you notice that typewriter on the desk in lounge? Wasn't Eileen Dawson's new will done on an old typewriter, and then supposedly signed by her?'

'Lots of older people have typewriters. It was probably Colin's mother's, before she passed away. The state of that place, I wouldn't be surprised if they had ten broken typewriters spread out over the house. If we arrested everyone with a typewriter somewhere in their home, we'd probably have half of Balloch Pass in custody.'

'It's worth investigating, though, don't you think?'

'I suppose, but you'll have to get a warrant.' Blair was defending any possibility of Colin and Noah's involvement, although she didn't know why. She'd cautioned Johnny time and time again against relying on gut feeling, but she'd never felt it so strongly before. If there was someone responsible for Eileen Dawson's death, she felt sure it wasn't them.

5

Noah had a list of house calls to make, and driving around the roads that surrounded Balloch Pass was a welcome relief from the scrutiny he was subjected to in town. He was almost getting used to walking into a shop and having the conversation stop, or change to another subject after an awkward pause. Most people were still pleasant enough to him, at least to his face, but there were enough who clearly believed the ongoing police investigation was a case of there being no smoke without fire.

It was bad enough that he needed permission just to leave town, but the refusal of some patients to see him, putting more pressure on Evie and Alasdair, was the worst thing of all.

At least none of the patients on his rounds so far had slammed the door in his face. It was hard enough for patients to secure a home visit these days, but he hadn't missed the fact that none of them had been on their own. Even Mrs Hargreaves, who was well into her nineties, and had always prided herself on managing alone, had dragged a neighbour in to be there when Noah arrived. Maybe he was reading too much into it, but it was a depressing thought. Especially if the investigation dragged on for months.

Pulling up to Drumcarling Farm, Noah swerved to miss the kamikaze chicken running across the farmyard, followed closely by a black-and-white sheepdog that looked hell-bent on helping itself to lunch.

'Here boy.' Getting out of the car, Noah called to the dog, which shot him a look and continued its chase of the chicken. The bird was making a pitiful sound, and flapping desperately a few feet into the air, before coming back down to the ground again. If Noah didn't intervene, all there'd be to show for the chase would be a mess of feathers and a dog with a well-rounded belly.

Slamming the door of the car, he crossed the farm yard, dodging the puddles left by a recent downpour, and positioned himself between the dog and the chicken. 'Come on boy, the game's up, I'm not going to let you eat her.' The dog wasn't going to give up easily, though, and he made one more lunge for the chicken, so Noah had to reach out and grab his collar, his wrist twisting as the dog fought against being restrained.

'Let's get you indoors, where you can't do any more harm.' The dog's spine was poking up through his coat. No wonder the poor thing was so determined to get a chicken dinner. The farmyard looked neglected, too. Fraser Daniels had been suffering with MS for the last ten years, but his records suggested he'd deteriorated quite significantly in the past year and, from the looks of things, he could use more than medical help.

Pulling up a loose piece of baling twine that was partly submerged in a dirty puddle, Noah slipped it through the hook on the dog's collar, the Collie looking up at him with soulful eyes. If Fraser agreed to it, he'd drive back into Balloch Pass and pick up some dog food. He couldn't leave the dog looking like this.

Noah lifted the knocker on the farmhouse door. Paint was peeling off the wood, making it almost bare in parts — another indicator of neglect.

'Mr Daniels, it's Dr Bradshaw. I'm here for your home visit.'

'What are you doing with my dog?' Fraser Daniels opened the window to the side of the door, a restrictor creating just enough gap to talk through, with the rest of him visible through the glass. His stomach was hanging over a pair of dirty tracksuit bottoms, the shirt having risen up, and his skin was mottled red and white — like a three day old slice of corned beef.

'He was chasing a chicken across the farmyard, so I thought it was best to bring him in. We need to give him a good feed, though, so he's not tempted again.'

'You're that doctor they're all talking about down in the town, aren't you? Ruby Henry called me up and told me all about it.'

'I see.' It was a shame Ruby hadn't taken the trouble to come and visit Fraser, to see if she could help him in a more practical way than just spreading gossip. The community were letting Fraser down, and now it didn't look like he was going to let Noah in. 'You rang about a change in your vision?'

'Aye, but it'll wait until one of the other doctors can get out. It's nothing serious.'

'I'd like to come in, to see if you're okay and make sure you've got enough in to feed yourself and the dog.'

'I'll not be letting you in Doctor, not with what they're all saying down in the town. I can't risk it, being on my own.'

Fraser shook his head, almost apologetically. 'But you're right about Stanley, I can't look after him like I used to. *I'm* happy to wait to see someone else, but I think it's time I accepted that Stanley needs someone else to look after him.'

'Does that mean you want me to take the dog?'

'If you can drop him off to the vets in town, they'll be able to find him a new home.'

'Are you certain you don't want me to take a look at you? I can't guarantee that one of the other doctors can get out today.'

'I'll take my chances.' Fraser pulled the window shut. Conversation over. So that was it: another patient was turning Noah away and risking their health, rather than trusting him to take care of them. Lifting Stanley into the back of his car, the dog's ribs were obvious to the touch. He'd do what he could to help the dog, and Fraser in a roundabout way, but whatever Evie and Alasdair said, this situation couldn't continue. If Blair didn't clear his name soon, it would be too late.

* * *

'Are you sure he's well enough to be questioned today?' Blair turned to Bill, as they waited outside the interview room. She didn't want Johnny involved in questioning Colin Hendry after his previous attempt, and she'd briefed Bill that they needed to take a different approach. The last thing she wanted was to have to call another ambulance.

'The doctor has given him the go ahead, and he elected not to have legal representation.'

'But he's got an appropriate adult with him instead then, hasn't he?' Blair wouldn't question Colin without one, whether he wanted it or not. He might not be a minor, but he was definitely a vulnerable adult, and she wanted him to have all the support he could get.

'Yes, they're both in there already.'

Bill took hold of the door handle. 'Let's get this done.'

'How are you feeling, Colin?' Blair smiled at him, as they entered the room, and he nodded in response.

'Better, thank you.'

'That's good. And you're sure you're ready to go ahead with the interview today?' Colin nodded again and Bill set up the recording, reeling off the caution, making Colin respond with a sharp intake of breath.

'Don't worry, we just want to ask you a few more questions about the last time you saw Eileen, and whether there was anything she said that can help us find out what happened, and whether anyone needs to be held to account for their actions.' Blair kept her gaze fixed firmly on his face. 'Is that clear to you, Colin, or do you need me to explain anything to you again?'

'I understand you, but I can't believe anyone would hurt Eileen. But if they did, I want to help f-f-find out who they are.'

'Are you aware that we've removed a typewriter from your house for forensic testing, to check whether it's the same type used to produce the new version of Eileen's will?'

'The other policeman told me that, but I don't know anything about it, and I don't remember it b-b-being there before. My mother had lots of old things around the house and if they didn't interest me, I didn't really n-n-notice them.'

'So, you're telling me you could have something like that in your house, for almost a year after your mother's death, and not even notice it was there?' Bill raised his eyebrows.

'I'm not much of cleaner, and I don't like to move her things around, she w-w-wouldn't like it.'

It seemed an odd thing to say given that his mother had been gone for some time, but Blair had seen for herself what a state the house was in, with junk piled everywhere like a hoarder's den. So it wasn't beyond the realms of possibility that he was telling the truth. 'You told us the other day that Eileen never mentioned leaving anything in her will to Dr Bradshaw or Father Douglas?'

'No, but even if she'd tried to talk to me about it, I'd have st-st-stopped her. I don't like talking about death, especially since I lost Ma.' Tears filled his eyes, and Blair wished he had someone with him who could give him a hug. Noah was right; the poor man had been through enough already.

'I'm sorry if this is difficult for you. But perhaps you can tell us whether Eileen talked much about how things were with her family?'

'She said she didn't see as much of her family as she'd like, and she missed my mother too. They were b-b-best friends, you know?' Colin smiled through the tears. 'It's why we liked to spend time together, but she was t-t-talking about moving in with her youngest daughter who lives in Edinburgh and c-c-couldn't visit much.'

'And how did you feel about that?' Blair kept her tone deliberately gentle.

'I was sad, and I didn't want her to go, but I knew it would make her h-h-happy.'

'Did she say *anything* about Father Douglas or Dr Bradshaw?' Bill tapped his fingers on the desk, the interview obviously progressing too slowly for his liking.

'She liked them both a lot. They were g-g-good to her and to me too. I don't know how I'd have c-c-coped after losing Ma, and then Eileen, without them.' Colin shook his head. 'I know some people are saying Dr Bradshaw might have k-k-killed her, but he wouldn't and you shouldn't listen to them that say he would.'

'We don't base any of our decisions on hearsay.' Blair leant forward slightly in her chair. 'But these are very serious accusations, and we need to check out all the information carefully.'

'I can't bear the thought of Dr Bradshaw going to prison. When Father

Douglas retires, he'll b-b-be all I have left.'

'Father Douglas is retiring?' Blair glanced at the one way panel of glass, hiding the room where Johnny and Chrissie were observing the interview.

'Yes, he's going after Christmas.' Colin's eyes filled with tears all over again but if he'd said nothing else of use during the interview, he'd already given them some important new information. If Father Douglas was retiring, and leaving behind the house which was tied to the job, he might suddenly find that money was a far more pressing issue. At the very least, the fact he hadn't mentioned it was odd . . . There'd been nothing in what Colin said to suggest Noah's involvement, though. So maybe she could still trust her gut after all.

* * *

'What did you make of that?' Blair was in the briefing room with Bill and

Chrissie, and Johnny had disappeared to take a call.

'Do you think he could have killed Eileen when he found out she was leaving?' Chrissie furrowed her brow, as if even she couldn't buy into the theory she was putting forward.

'I very much doubt it.' Blair was more certain than ever that Colin had nothing to do with Eileen's death. He was a vulnerable and lonely man, who had leant on his mother's best friend for support after his bereavement, so the last thing he'd want was to lose her forever too. Eileen had only *mentioned* the possibility of leaving, in any case, and Colin struck Blair as someone who would hold onto every shred of hope for as long as he could. 'I'm more interested in why Father Douglas didn't tell us he was retiring. He might have shared his inheritance with the church in the past, but that puts a different spin on it this time. Maybe he realised he was going to need to get his hands on some money, and fast.'

'Surely the Church looks after its priests when they retire?' Bill sucked his cheeks in. 'I really can't believe Father Douglas had a strong enough motive to go against everything he believed in.'

'Sorry about that.' Johnny's face was flushed as he tore into the room. 'But it was forensics; there's been a development.'

'Well come on, spit it out, son.' Bill could be impatient with Johnny, but Blair was with him this time.

'They've confirmed that the typewriter we seized from Colin's place is the same model as the one used to type up Eileen's altered will. Apparently they can tell by the typeface. They're going to do some more tests now, to see whether they can pull some fingerprints from it, or identify for sure if it was the one used to rewrite the will, by analysing imprints on the ribbon.'

'Do you think they stand any chance? There's so much dust in his house, I can't believe any of the stuff on those shelves has been used for years. And the ribbon must be thirty or forty years old, if it's an original.' Blair shook her head.

'I don't know, but I think we need to get Colin back in again and ask him about it. I think it was brushed over in the first interview.' Johnny gave Bill a look. Blair would have to watch those two.

'But if Colin's typewriter was used to change the will, then why wouldn't he change it to favour himself?' Blair couldn't shake the feeling that they were heading in the wrong direction by focusing on Colin. Even if this didn't turn out to be murder, there was a good chance that Eileen hadn't changed the will herself, which meant someone had committed fraud. The chances of that being Colin seemed incredibly remote.

'Maybe his motive was his relationship with Father Douglas and Dr Bradshaw?' Chrissie cocked her head to one side. 'I get the feeling that he might . . . you know . . . *bat for the other side*.'

'I think calling that a motive is a stretch, even if he does have those sort of feelings for one of them.' Blair would have to talk to Chrissie later about the way she'd described Colin's sexuality, but they had other priorities for now. 'He clearly saw Eileen as a replacement mother figure, and I think that would have overridden anything else.'

'There's always a possibility that one of them manipulated him, so he felt he had no choice?' Johnny met her gaze. 'I know you're convinced Colin's innocent, and I don't think he's capable of murder either . . . But he could have been coerced into being an accomplice — changing the will and planting it at Eileen's place, either before or after her death.'

'So what you're saying is that we're no closer to knowing anything for sure?' Chrissie looked as deflated as Blair felt. Her senior officer was pushing for an update, and she'd have to make a recommendation before too long about whether the case should be referred on. They needed to find some critical evidence. And soon.

* * *

Noah led Stanley into the veterinary surgery, pulling hard on the piece of baling twine still threaded through the loop on his collar. He might not look as though he'd seen a vet in a long time, but the dog definitely wasn't keen to go inside.

'Come on, boy. Help me out a bit. I promise this is for the best.' When his words of encouragement made no difference, Noah was forced to drag the dog through the door, and up to the reception desk.

'Hi, I'm Dr Noah Bradshaw. I went out on a home visit to see Fraser Daniels and he told me that his dog, Stanley, is registered here?'

'I can't really give out that sort of information.' The young woman sitting behind the desk looked him up and down. 'You know, data protection and all that.'

'Can you at least get someone to look at the dog? You can see he hasn't been looked after as well as he should have been recently, and Fraser has admitted he can't cope with him anymore. He asked me to bring him here so that you can find someone to rehome him.' Noah wasn't going to admit that was *all* Fraser had permitted him to do. He was good enough to look after a dog, but apparently not trustworthy enough to treat a patient. Maybe he should enquire about a job whilst he was here.

'We don't do rehoming ourselves, but we could contact the rescue centre. Although I know they're inundated at the moment, and they're having to have dogs *put down*.' She whispered the words, as if Stanley might be able to understand them.

'Can someone take a look at him, please?' He wanted to make sure that the dog wasn't about to drop dead before they worried about the challenge of rehoming him. It would do even less for Noah's reputation if Stanley didn't make it through an hour in his company.

'I'll ask Sarah if she can have a look. She's due to go home after she's finished with Minky, the cat she's seeing now, but she'll probably be willing to take a look, if you can take a seat in the waiting area? Jasper's got back-to-back appointments, so if Sarah can't see you before she leaves, you might have to come back at the end of surgery, instead.'

'Okay.' It wasn't as if Noah had anything better to do. He dragged a reluctant Stanley into the waiting area, where two rows of black chairs with PVC-covered seats faced each other. There were four shelves, filled with different types of dog and cat food, on the end wall of the waiting area. Noah had no idea there were so many variations of dog food targeted to meet the needs of specific breeds, sizes and ages of dog, but poor Stanley would probably have gobbled up any type of food. As he sat down, the dog looked up at him, whining. Stanley turned two circles and then sat directly on top of Noah's feet.

There was one other couple in the waiting room with something hissing from inside a pet carrier, which he could only assume was a cat. The woman whispered to the man next to her, who shot Noah a none-too-subtle glance. Even as a kid, he'd never wanted to be famous, knowing he couldn't stand the public scrutiny. And his current level of notoriety was his idea of hell. He picked up one of the leaflets about pet cremation and turned the picture away so Stanley couldn't see it. He was getting as bad as the receptionist already. It wasn't a subject he anticipated ever needing to know about, but it gave him something to read. Anything so he wouldn't have to look up and see the woman, or her partner, staring at him again.

'Sarah can see you now, if you can

bring Stanley through, please?' The young receptionist had walked through to the waiting area, and was looking at him expectantly.

'Come on, Stanley. They just want to check you out.' Noah stood up, but this time the dog absolutely refused to budge, despite him pulling on the baling twine. 'Come on, or I'm just going to carry you in there.' Stanley gave him another of his doleful looks, and Noah had no choice but to scoop the dog into his arms. He was far lighter than he should have been, and his rib cage pressed into Noah's chest.

'If you can just put him down on there, please.' The vet gestured to the examination table as Noah came into the room with Stanley in his arms. Thankfully the dog wasn't fighting him anymore. The poor thing probably didn't have the energy.

'Tara said the owner asked you to bring the dog in, for him to be sent to the rehoming centre?'

'Yes, that's right. Fraser says he can't

cope with the dog anymore and, looking at him, I'm inclined to agree.' Noah held on tightly to Stanley's collar, just in case the dog found the energy to make a dash for freedom. 'There are still a few chickens up at the farm and they look okay, but it's maybe worth someone making a welfare visit up there to check them out too.'

'I can ask Tara to contact the RSPCA, but as for Stanley here, I think his best hope is to go to the rehoming centre. Although in his current state, and at his age, the odds are against him.'

'Is he past help?' Noah didn't know if Stanley was still up for it, but he suddenly felt like making a dash for it with the dog. He hadn't saved him only for the poor thing to end his days at the rescue centre because no one wanted to rehome him.

'No, he's not quite that bad yet, but it looks like you got to him just in time.' Whilst she'd been talking, the vet had listened to his heart, pinched the loose skin on his back, and begun to run her hands over him, looking into his ears and eyes. 'He's very thin, but at least he's not dehydrated, because his skin is still pinging back when I pinch it. There's no obvious sign of illness or disease, either. We'll need to run some blood tests just to be sure, but we can leave him in the kennels here overnight, and see if the rescue centre will take him tomorrow.'

'And if they can't?'

'If the blood tests show he needs any ongoing treatment then he may have to be put down.' Maybe Noah's imagination was playing tricks on him, but he could have sworn the dog flattened itself closer to the examination table as the vet spoke. He shouldn't feel responsible for a dog he'd known nothing about an hour earlier, but he did.

'Can I take him? At least until we've got the results of the blood tests and we know what the situation with the rescue centre is?'

'It's not what we'd normally do.' The vet looked down at Stanley again and then back up at Noah. 'But if I call Stanley's registered owner, and he gives me his permission, then I don't see why not.'

'Thank you.' It was a crazy thing to offer. He didn't have time to look after a dog and, with the way things were, he might have to quit his job before the test results even came back. But he couldn't just walk away and leave Stanley to his fate.

Stanley barely reacted to the vet taking his blood, and Noah carried him out to the waiting area whilst she put in the call to Fraser Daniels. He just hoped that Stanley's owner would recognise what was best for the dog, even if he hadn't trusted Noah to step over the threshold of his home.

To Noah's relief, the couple who'd been waiting with their cat had gone in to see the other vet, so he was free to browse the shelves of dog food without them scrutinising his every move. He picked up a bag of food especially for senior dogs, which the vet had recommended to use little and often to gradually build Stanley's eating back up to normal levels. Paying the receptionist for it, he put it under his seat whilst they waited for Fraser's verdict. If he wasn't allowed to take Stanley home, he could at least send him on his way with a bag of food.

'Mr Daniels has okayed it for you to take Stanley home with you, and you can decide what to do next once we have the results of the blood tests. You should be able to ring up or pop in for those on Wednesday.' The vet smiled at him, no doubt relieved that the fate of the dog was out of her hands. 'And you're clear what to do about upping his food intake?'

'Yes, thanks.'

'You might want to take this until you can get your own lead.' She handed him a blue leash. 'It's from a dog we had in to put down earlier in the week, but I don't suppose Stanley will mind too much.'

'I don't suppose he will.' Noah clipped the lead onto the dog and led him out towards the exit, Stanley suddenly finding a turn of speed he hadn't thought possible. 'Thanks very much for your help.'

Lifting Stanley on to the back seat of the car, Noah cursed under his breath. He'd left the bag of dog food under his seat in the waiting area.

'Sorry boy, I won't be a minute. I'm just going to go in and get your food.' Was he going to turn into one of *those* people straight away? The sort who had conversations with their dog. Maybe he'd been on his own too long. An image of DI Blair Hannah suddenly flitted into his mind, but he shook his head. The responsibility of a dog, even if it was only for a week, was more than enough for now. And what woman in her right mind would want to get involved with someone under suspicion for murder anyway? Let alone the detective leading the case.

Noah pushed open the door to the veterinary surgery and caught just enough of the conversation between the vet and her receptionist before they saw him to know that the rumours about his involvement with Eileen Dawson's death were still going strong.

' . . . doesn't really matter, if he does, as the dog was probably doomed to being put down anyway. So it would just be trading one lethal injection for another.'

'I forgot the food.' Noah said, making the vet's head jerk up in surprise.

'I'm sorry, we were just . . . '

'Yeah, I know. You were just jumping to the same conclusions as half the population of Balloch Pass.' He could have said a lot more — got angry and protested his innocence. But, like Stanley, he was just too tired. Sometimes you had to accept when you were beaten, and maybe it was time.

* * *

'I'm sorry. The last thing I wanted was for Evie to have to go out and make a house call.'

'We thought it was best if she went and checked Fraser out, to make sure the issues with his eyes are related to the progression of the MS and nothing new. But I think she was actually grateful for the chance to get away from the house for a bit. She's going stir crazy since she cut down her hours even more, and I've got no idea how she's going to cope when she's off altogether after the baby. I can see us working out some sort of job share before too long. Although I quite like the idea of staying at home with the baby and watching daytime TV!'

'I don't think it works like that! You'll be begging to go back to work for a rest, after a couple of weeks.' Noah looked over to where Alasdair's god-daughter, Bronte, was gently brushing Stanley's fur, while her brother, Rory, told him all about after-school football practice. 'The dog certainly seems to be a hit with the kids. Maybe you should take him, if I have to leave.' Noah fought to keep his tone casual.

'I've already told you that you can't do that. It took us far too long to find a doctor we wanted to work with. I know things aren't perfect at the moment, but I trust the police to get to the bottom of this, and we're more than happy to ride out the storm until then to keep you with us.'

'Maybe you should suspend me without pay until the police decide if there's a case to answer. That way you could afford to get a locum in. You can't keep paying me if half the patients have no confidence in me.'

'And what sort of message would that send out? I spoke to the Board and they've got no concerns about your suitability to continue practising. You haven't been charged, and all three of us have been questioned, so we'd all have to quit on that basis. I think, for your own sake, we should take you off home visits for now. But we can manage that, along with support from the on-call network, if we need to.' Alasdair put a hand on his shoulder.

'Just promise me you won't do anything stupid like disappearing without saying anything.'

'No chance. I can't even leave town without notifying the police of my movements.' Noah's laugh was hollow. He'd stay until Stanley's situation was sorted, but if the police weren't able to vindicate him by then, it didn't matter what Alasdair and Evie said. It was time to go.

6

When Blair told her father she was in the middle of a murder investigation, before they'd found enough evidence to decide that, it wasn't because she shared Johnny's burning desire to see the case turn into one — it was just a way of holding off the inevitable guilt-driven meet up. The get-togethers were always uncomfortable; they'd often stare across the table at one another in silence, like they had most evenings after her mother died, before she'd finally been able to escape to university three years later. The silence would be interrupted every now and then, with stilted attempts to keep the conversation going. They were like two participants in an ill-matched blind date, where every awkward silence seemed magnified ten-fold. That was the best case scenario, though. These days, it was more likely that her father would start to lecture her about his latest idea of what was best for her, bringing a whole new meaning to the term *silence is golden*. It was a lose-lose situation. So calling Eileen Dawson's death a murder investigation had been purely for Blair's convenience. Until the call came in.

'There's been another unexpected death in Balloch Pass — a middle aged man called Fraser Daniels.' Chrissie knocked on her door, but barely waited for a response before rushing in. 'The Procurator Fiscal requested an immediate autopsy as soon as it was called in by Dr Evie James. She's one of the GPs at the Balloch Pass surgery.'

'And have they got any news on the outcome yet?'

'Only the preliminary results, but apparently there's an obvious injection site near the deceased's armpit, and the initial toxicology report shows evidence of Rohypnol in his system.'

'The tranquilizer?' Blair had encountered a few cases where the drug had been used to subdue victims of sexual assault, but she'd never encountered it in a potential murder. 'I take it that it hadn't been prescribed to him?'

'Not according to Dr James. He also had high levels of potassium, like Eileen Dawson. But this time they can't be written off as a result of damage to the heart muscle.' Chrissie paused, like a comedian timing the punch line. 'Because there were obvious traces of potassium chloride in his system, and the pathologist is almost sure the death was due to a deliberate overdose.'

'The pathologist told us there was a remote possibility of that being Eileen's cause of death, too.' Blair picked up her mobile phone. 'I think we can be almost certain now that she *was* murdered. There are just too many coincidences. Do we know who the last person to see Mr Daniels was?'

'No, but Dr James said she'd seen him two nights before his death, after he refused a home visit from Noah Bradshaw. And the pathologist said he'd only been dead a matter of hours before Dr James found him. So that means he was probably killed on Saturday afternoon, or late Saturday morning at the earliest.'

'It sounds like that puts Noah Bradshaw in the frame again, then. Get Bill and Johnny to bring him in for questioning.' Blair gestured to the phone. 'And I'll give the Chief Inspector a call, it might be time to turn this one over.' It was standard protocol, but she would have done it anyway. If Noah was involved, then her belief in his innocence might just have cost Fraser Daniels his life.

* * *

'What do you mean you've let him go?' Blair had just got back from a meeting, where she'd assured senior officers that the prime suspect was in custody, and now Bill was telling her that they'd already released Noah Bradshaw.

'We didn't have a lot of choice Boss, he was six hundred miles away at the time of the murder, in London. We'd had a call from the Met to confirm it.'

'How do the Met know his whereabouts?' There'd been no time to gather CCTV, and Noah's alibi couldn't be taken at face value. So why was the Greater London police force corroborating it? None of it made any sense.

'He was with Superintendent Andrew Collins for the whole weekend. From when he arrived on Friday morning — after driving down overnight on Thursday — until he left on Sunday morning, after the body had already been discovered. He'd put a call in to the station too, to say he'd be away for a few days, and the address he gave was in London.' Bill looked at his notes. 'Unless he's got a senior officer from the Met lying for him, then it couldn't have been Bradshaw. But we've been on to the surveillance teams anyway, to get hold of the CCTV, just to make sure.'

'None of this adds up. Why on earth would he drive all that way to spend a day and a half with a Superintendent from the Met? Do we know what their relationship is?' Blair couldn't trust her judgement around Noah Bradshaw, and there was still a chance that this was all just some elaborate cover up. But that sort of stuff was for TV shows, surely? Not real life.

'They're brothers-in-law. At least they were before Bradshaw's wife passed away eighteen months ago.' Bill shrugged. 'I know you want to make this fit, but I think we're barking up the wrong tree with this one.'

'I'm not trying to make anything fit.' Blair's scalp prickled. Bill should know her better than that. 'Let's not jump to any conclusions either way, until we know for sure. I want Chrissie on the case to make sure we get hold of the CCTV as soon as possible. That way, we can either rule Bradshaw out altogether, or bring him back in. The Chief Inspector has put in a request to move the case to one of the Major Investigation Teams as soon as she can. But, in the meantime, we can't afford to let anything, *or anyone*, slip through our fingers.'

⋆ ⋆ ⋆

'Did they call you in for questioning too?' Noah's eyes ached from the lack of sleep he'd had over the past few days. It had been enough that he'd driven down to London and back in the space of about seventy-two hours, and spent the time down there going over old ground with Andrew and the rest of Katie's family until late at night. But being hauled into the police station for questioning as soon as he got back had just about finished him off.

'It was only informal questioning, at the hospital after I found the body. Then again, back at the surgery, when they were checking up on your story.' Evie spoke as Alasdair handed them both a drink. The children were in bed and Stanley was curled up on a rug in front of the dormant fireplace, as if he could will it to ignite with sheer desire.

'My *story*?' Noah didn't doubt that Alasdair and Evie were on his side, but just the word seemed to suggest that he was trying to cover something up.

'I'm sorry, you know what I mean. They just seemed to find it difficult to believe you'd take Stanley and drive all that way for just a couple of nights.' Evie ran a hand over her growing bump. 'But when I told them why you were visiting, they seemed a bit more convinced.'

'So going to my dead wife's thirtieth birthday party gives me a get out of jail free card?' He hated the fact that he was having to play on Katie's death to clear his name. Seeing her family again, and the raw grief they were all still going through, had been like a kick in the gut. Because he didn't feel it, not in the same way. If he ever cleared his name, there might well be another wife for him, one day — a new start. But Doug and Paula would never have another daughter, and Andrew had lost his only sister. If he'd really loved Katie, like a husband should love a wife, then he could have shared their grief properly. But playing along had made him feel like the worst kind of fraud. Maybe the guilt written on his face was making Blair Hannah and her team determined that he was behind Eileen and Fraser's deaths. But telling Katie's family the truth to unburden his conscience would just have hurt them more. So he'd keep his secret, however hard that was.

'It's all complete rubbish, Noah, but they will get to that conclusion eventually.' Alasdair put an arm around Evie as he spoke. I think it was a good thing you went back to London and saw Katie's family, though. You needed to get away from this place for a bit, before it all got too much.'

'I'm glad you persuaded me to go. I was ready to leave altogether after Fraser refused to see me, but speaking to Andrew about the process of these types of investigations has given me new hope that they might get there in the end.' Noah took a sip of his drink. 'And it'd just look even worse if I left.'

'Surely they know it isn't you?' Evie screwed up her face. 'You weren't even in Scotland when Fraser died, let alone in Balloch Pass.'

'You'd think so, but apparently even a Superintendent's word isn't worth anything, unless it's backed up by CCTV.'

'It'll be alright. By the end of next week, they'll have it all sorted. I'm sure of it.' Evie smiled. It had been said before and he wanted to believe her, more than anything. But sometimes things didn't work out as they should. Katie's death had been proof enough of that.

* * *

As expected, the CCTV footage confirmed Noah's story. His car had been parked outside his brother-in-law's house in Hampstead the entire weekend, and he'd also been captured on

CCTV footage outside restaurants and shops in the area, walking his dog. There was hardly a window of six hours between the sightings, even overnight. So, unless he'd hired a helicopter or a private plane to fly back and murder Fraser Daniels, it wasn't him. And if he didn't kill Fraser, the likelihood was that he'd had nothing to do with Eileen's death either. Blair had received notification that both deaths were now being treated as murder, and the new team would be looking again at other unexpected deaths over the past few years. The killer had made a mistake with Fraser — the obvious injection site, and the clear evidence of toxins in the body, ruled this one out as a heart attack. And it might prove to be just the start.

'Whoever is doing this is getting sloppy, or maybe they want to get caught.' Blair had agreed with the Chief Inspector that her team would carry on conducting interviews in Balloch Pass, until the Major Investigation Team were ready to proceed. They were coming to the end of a high profile case involving a member of parliament, and they couldn't take over until the Procurator Fiscal had agreed there was enough evidence to charge all the suspects. The entire force were pushed to the limit, and the Chief Inspector had admitted the situation was less than ideal. But, with Blair's experience, her team were the next best thing. At least that was how she'd sold it to her, but she couldn't help thinking that a small town like Balloch Pass was always going to be pushed to the back of the queue, even if they had a potential serial killer on their hands.

'Have you considered another possibility?' Johnny stopped chewing on the end of his pen as he spoke. 'It might not be down to sloppiness, it could be that there are two different killers. Maybe Bradshaw *did* kill Eileen, and got someone else to kill Fraser, while he had a rock solid alibi, to put himself in the clear for both murders.'

'Like who?' Bill's tone was sharp. He was old school, and conspiracy theories definitely weren't his thing.

'I don't know. One of the other doctors?'

'So now you think the three of them are in on it?' Bill actually laughed this time. 'I'm sorry to disappoint you Johnny-Boy, but they were both at the hospital all day, after they thought their godson had broken his arm. It was only when they finally got home, that Evie decided to go back and check on Fraser Daniels again. Even if she killed him the second she got there, the timelines just don't fit in with the pathologist's report.'

'It could have been someone easier to manipulate, then, like Colin Hendry.'

'It wasn't Colin.' Blair didn't have to rely on her gut this time. 'He's got an even more solid alibi than the James' and Noah Bradshaw, because he was *here*. He came in voluntarily for further questioning, with a legal aid representative this time, so he could make an official statement. The solicitor met with him beforehand, and the interview here didn't conclude until late afternoon.'

'But there's still the issue of the typewriter.' Johnny tapped his pen on the table. 'If the tests show it definitely was the one used to re-write Eileen Dawson's will, then surely that puts Colin Hendry back in the frame for *her* murder?'

'We'll deal with that when we come to it. But looking at the facts we know about Colin at the moment, there's nothing to suggest his involvement — other than malicious gossip.'

'Which means we're nearly a month into this, and we're no further forward than we were?' Johnny looked like a kid who'd dropped his ice cream. He was learning the hard way that this was how it was sometimes — two steps forward and one-and-a-half back.

'We have made some progress. We can rule a few people out now, and go back out there and speak to the community again with a new focus.' Blair wasn't sure if she was trying to convince Johnny or herself. But, whatever the reason, she wanted to hand the investigation over with more than they had. 'Chrissie and Bill, I want you to see if you can track down any of Fraser Daniels' family members, and speak to Eileen Dawson's family again. See if you can find out whether there's any connection between the two of them that might lead us to other suspects. Janey, can you and the others go back through the interview transcripts and case notes we've put together so far, to see if we've missed anything by focussing on Noah Bradshaw and Colin Hendry? And, Johnny, I need you to work with me, again. I'll meet you in my office in ten minutes and I'll brief you on the action plan then.'

* * *

The one upside of having fewer patients willing to see him was that Noah could spend longer with those brave — or desperate — enough to risk an appointment with him. Aggie Green was next on his list, and he was actually looking forward to seeing her. She could be outspoken and maybe even a bit brash at times, but there'd be no sideways glances at him to see if he was acting like someone capable of murder. She was the sort of woman who believed what she believed, and nothing could sway her from that. Thank goodness she still seemed to believe in him.

'How has the tiredness been since you started taking the iron supplements?' Noah looked at her notes as she sat down in his consulting room. She'd come in almost three weeks before to see if she had anaemia, and the blood tests had shown that her iron level was a bit low.

'A bit better, but folk keep telling me it's my age and I should expect it. Only this morning, Father Douglas told me I should retire when he does. Now that I've not got the post office any more, he thinks I'm ready to be put out to pasture!'

'I'm sure that's not what he thinks.' If Father Douglas had said that out loud, then he was a much braver man than Noah. 'I take it you've not had any luck with the petition, then?'

'I'm still collecting signatures, Doctor, but I've had people refuse and say they can get their stamps online. It wasn't just about stamps and the like, though, it was the heart of the community.'

'I agree and it's a real shame, but sadly things do move on sometimes. And I'm worried that if you fixate all your energy on this and end up disappointed, you could get really run down.'

'Now you sound exactly like Father Douglas! What the pair of you don't realise is that I'm big enough and ugly enough to look after myself.'

'Okay, point taken. But I know you still do a lot for the community, even though you aren't running the post office any more. If you make yourself ill, how do you think those people are going to be able to cope without you?'

'I could say the same of you, Doctor. It's about time those incompetent detectives found out who's really behind Fraser and Eileen's deaths.' Aggie shook her head. 'And I know you're going to tell me off for this, but my money is still on Colin. He's not been right in the head since his mother died, and that sort of thing can make people do funny things.'

'Colin needs support, not fingers pointed at him, and I'm confident the police will clear us both completely before too long.' Noah wasn't going to get into another argument with her about Colin. She'd made up her mind and there was no changing it. All he could do was hope there weren't too many people in Balloch Pass like that, or the mud currently being slung at both him and Colin would stick for good too.

* * *

'Come in, Johnny.' Blair gestured to the seat on the opposite side of the desk.

'What's up, Boss? Bill reckons I'm in for a telling off.' Johnny looked as if the thought bothered him.

'Why? Have you done something to deserve one?'

'It's not always easy to tell.' Johnny dropped his gaze. 'But I'm enjoying learning from the best, even if it's not an easy ride.'

'Nothing worth doing is ever easy.' Blair dug her fingernails into the palm of her hand, trying not to think about the last time she'd lost her patience with Johnny. He'd made a minor mistake and not followed up a phone call with the Procurator Fiscal's Office before they'd shut for the night. But it hadn't been the end of the world, and the real reason she'd flown at him was because of the pressure she was getting from her dad about when they could meet. There'd been a long voicemail from her father, describing in great detail how disappointed he was with her attitude — as if she hadn't heard it all before. A hundred times, probably. And Johnny had borne the brunt of that, because he was there and because he'd made enough of a mistake for her to get away with it.

'I know that, and I want to be the best detective I can be, but I know there's still a lot to learn. So if you've got me in here to bring me down to earth, I'm sure that'll cheer Bill up.'

'I think it's hard for him to see you arrive with so much ambition, and know that one day he might have to call you 'Boss'.' Blair shrugged. 'But that's not why I wanted to see you. I need your help with something.'

'I'm listening.'

'Now that we know Noah Bradshaw had nothing to do with Fraser Daniels' death, and almost certainly had no involvement with Eileen Dawson's death, I want to make sure that everyone knows. Balloch Pass is a small community and gossip spreads fast about the changes to Eileen's will, mostly because of her family I suspect. But however it got out there, it seems to have been enough to convince some people of Noah's guilt and I want that to change.'

'You quite like him, don't you?' Johnny was pushing his luck, and the look on his face suggested he knew it.

'It's not too late for me to shout at you.' Blair shuffled some papers on the desk, so she wouldn't have to look at him. He was right, she did like Noah. She admired his straight-up responses to her questions, and the fact that he wasn't prepared to let the community make Colin Hendry a scapegoat — even when that had left him firmly in the frame. But this wasn't about whether she liked him or not, this was about what was best for the community. 'I want his name cleared because it's a small rural town with limited access to medical services, and if half the population are refusing to see the only full-time doctor, then it could have serious repercussions. Whoever is responsible for

Fraser and Eileen's deaths, we don't want more blood on *our* hands.'

'Agreed, but how are we supposed to stop all the rumours without making an arrest?'

'We need to find someone who's capable of spreading the news that both Noah Bradshaw and Colin Hendry have been discounted from our inquiries.' Blair looked at her notes again. 'I think Aggie Green would be a good starting point, and the woman she was with in the market that day, Janet, wasn't it?'

'I think her name was Janet Blake. She and Aggie certainly seemed capable of pointing the finger at Colin, and spreading those rumours in the first place, so they should be able to put out the opposite message — if they want to, that is. But I'm not sure I could infiltrate the WI, or wherever it is they hang out, without raising a few eyebrows.'

'Do I need to book you into some refresher training on equality and diversity with Chrissie, after her comments about the possibility of Colin being gay? Making stereotypes about women of a certain age isn't much better.' Blair couldn't help laughing at the look on his face.

'Oh please, no, anything but that.'

'Good, and there's no need to infiltrate the WI or anywhere else. All I'm asking you to do is to work the connections you've made, to make sure the message gets through to them.'

'What connections?' Johnny looked confused.

'Well you could start off by mentioning it at one of the regular meet-ups you've been having with their community police constable, Vicky.'

'I haven't . . . '

'Let me stop you before you really do get yourself into trouble, Johnny. One thing I won't tolerate from my team is lying. I know you've been seeing her socially, and that's none of my business, as long as you aren't sharing inappropriate details of the investigation with her.' Blair looked at him levelly. 'Except when I tell you to.'

'Right, so you want me to tell her that Hendry and Bradshaw are in the clear?'

'I want you to tell her exactly *why* they're in the clear, and let her know that, if anyone in the community asks how the investigation is going, she needs to tell them we've taken Hendry and Bradshaw off the list of possible suspects. I want you to find out more about Janet, too, to see how we can make sure this gets back to her. When we go and speak to Father Douglas again, I'm going to make sure he knows. And, if Aggie Green is there to overhear it, all the better.'

'I'll do my best, Boss.'

She nodded in response, confident he'd find a way to make it happen. They owed it to Noah Bradshaw, and the community, to make sure his name was cleared, but she'd have gone to the same lengths for anyone. She was almost sure of it.

7

Blair checked her mobile after she parked outside Father Douglas' house. A message from Bill or Chrissie, saying they'd uncovered a new lead, would have been very welcome. There was nothing, except six missed calls from her father, which he must have done one after the other. He'd obviously decided to leave a voicemail at some point during the stream of calls, but she slid the phone into her pocket without listening to it. Getting back to him could wait and even then, she'd stick to a text.

Johnny was in her good books, having managed to find out that Janet Blake worked in a charity shop in Balloch Pass. So the last thing he deserved was having his ear chewed off again because she was smarting from speaking to her father. Johnny had even arranged to take a dummy call on his mobile that morning when Janet was in the shop — having a one-sided conversation that made it perfectly clear Noah and Colin were off the suspect list. Janet would probably be spreading that information before she even finished her shift.

'Remind me why we're going to speak to Father Douglas again?' Johnny's eyes were bloodshot and, for once, he was the one who looked as if he'd been up all night.

'Because now that we've discounted Colin and Noah, we need to see if Father Douglas can tell us who else Eileen associated with, and we've never questioned him about Fraser Daniels or whether he was a regular at the church. I'm just hoping he was, because Chrissie and Bill haven't been able to uncover much else about him. Unfortunately for us, it looks like he kept himself more or less to himself.' Blair opened the car door. 'And with any luck we'll get a chance to talk to Aggie again, too. We might even find out if the information you fed Janet has reached her yet.'

Crossing the driveway, the gravel crunched under their feet and Father Douglas was at the door before they even reached it. Another man, who looked to be in his sixties, was just coming out of the house.

'Thank you for the tea, Father, and I'm glad to see you looking better. We were all worried about you when you missed choir practice on Saturday morning. It's so unlike you.'

'I just can't shake things off so easily at my age.' Father Douglas smiled. 'You'll have to excuse me though, Gerry. These nice young police detectives are here to see me.'

'You watch out for them, Father.' The man looked Blair up and down as he spoke. 'They all but had Doc Bradshaw hung, drawn and quartered for Eileen's murder, and now they've realised how wrong they were. They could save people a lot of heartache, if they got their facts straight first.'

'Now, now, Gerry, they're only doing their job, and getting their facts straight is what they're here for. You take care now and I'll see you for choir practice on Saturday.' Father Douglas waved his hand, ushering Blair and Johnny through the space on the other side of him, shutting the door behind them as soon as they crossed the threshold.

'I'm sorry about that, but with another suspicious death in the town, emotions are understandably running high, and everyone's a bit on edge.'

'Of course, and don't worry, Johnny and I have had far more abuse than that hurled at us in the past. It's an occupational hazard — sometimes you just can't do right for doing wrong.'

'Come through to the sitting room and I'll get you both a cup of tea. Sadly there's no Aggie today, so that means there's no cake either.' Father Douglas patted his stomach. 'She did make a Victoria sponge cake yesterday, but Gerry and I just saw off the last of that. Let me take your coats and you can go and get settled, whilst I see if I can still handle this kettle boiling business.'

For some reason, Johnny seemed to feel the need to whisper, even though Father Douglas had gone out to the kitchen to make drinks. 'That ruined your plan to speak to Aggie then, Boss.'

'It's okay. That guy on the doorstep seemed to know that Noah's in the clear, so it looks like Janet's been doing her thing.'

'Did you notice he said Father Douglas missed choir practice on *Saturday morning*?' Johnny had that look again, his quarry in his sights.

'I did, and it's something we'll need to ask him about.'

'Well, you'll be pleased to hear that I've rustled up some biscuits.' Father Douglas came back through the door to the sitting room with a heavily laden tray, which he set on the coffee table in front of Blair. 'Shall I be mother and pour?'

'Please.' The elderly man's hands were shaky as he raised the teapot up.

He didn't look like a man capable of committing two murders, but they couldn't rule him out completely. He was the only beneficiary in Eileen Dawson's altered will who they hadn't managed to discount from their inquiries yet. 'We just need to ask you a few more questions following Fraser Daniels' death, which the Procurator Fiscal's office have ruled as murder. It also means we're almost certain now that Eileen Dawson's death was murder too.'

'I never thought I'd see the day when Balloch Pass was embroiled in something like this. Two murders, and Fraser was only a young man, at least by my standards. Although everyone seems young when you reach your mid-seventies.'

'You're looking very good on it, Father.' Blair wanted him to feel relaxed; he was more likely to open up that way, but this wasn't false flattery. Father Douglas' face was almost entirely unlined and, despite his slight shakiness, he could have passed for a man much younger. But given that he was in his mid-seventies, it was no wonder he felt like he'd served his time in the church. She took a sip of the tea, which tasted as if the milk might be going off. Appearances could be deceptive and maybe Father Douglas had realised he needed someone to look after him when he left the priesthood and Aggie behind. Was the thought of paying for that enough of a motive to drive him to murder?

'Where were you on Saturday morning?' Johnny was taking the direct approach.

'Saturday mornings are always choir practice.' Father Douglas smiled and handed Johnny his cup. 'Would you like a biscuit?'

'No thanks.' Johnny took the cup, and shot Blair a look. She nodded to let him know he could go ahead. There was no point dragging things out at this stage of the investigation. They'd be handing it over soon, so they had to make every question count. 'Are you sure you were at choir practice this Saturday, Father?'

'Oh heavens, you're right, I wasn't!' Father Douglas' already rosy cheeks seemed to colour to a deeper shade of red. 'I had an appointment with . . . '

Blair didn't hear what he said next. The clatter of a cup and saucer on to the coffee table made her turn towards Johnny. His usually pale complexion was already dark red, and his hand had flown to his throat. She'd seen an anaphylactic shock once before, during an arrest — and Johnny was definitely having one. He hadn't touched the biscuits, all he'd had was the tea. But the colour on his face was rash-like — and it was spreading down his neck.

'Don't panic, Johnny. Where's your epi-pen?' He carried the injectable adrenaline at all times and she'd had training to administer it when he'd started on her team.

'Coat . . . pocket.' Johnny was already struggling to speak, and she fought to keep her voice level in response. All she wanted was for someone with the right training to take over, and for once she'd even have been happy to see her father show up.

'Father Douglas, I need Johnny's coat, quickly please.' The priest moved remarkably fast for a man of his age, and he was back at Blair's side within seconds.

'Thank you.' The first pocket was empty, and Blair held her breath as she plunged her hand into the second pocket. Nothing. 'Johnny, it's not there.'

'Must . . . be.' His breathing was getting more laboured, and she ran her hands all over the coat, shaking it, just in case the epi-pen was hidden in some secret inside pocket.

'I'll call an ambulance.' Father Douglas had his hands knitted together, as if he was already silently praying for a miracle. But Blair wasn't about to leave this in the hands of some other worldly force she wasn't even sure existed. Johnny needed help right now.

'Get the ambulance to go to the

doctor's surgery. I've got to get him there if he's going to . . . ' She wanted to say 'stand a chance', but if she'd said the words out loud it would have made them true, and it would have made Johnny panic even more. 'I've got to get him there, so they can sort him out.'

'Of course.' Father Douglas moved over to the telephone, which was on a desk in one corner of the room. She couldn't wait for him to finish the call — she had to move Johnny now — and she wasn't sure if Father Douglas would be more of a hindrance than a help, anyway.

'Come on Johnny, we've got to get you in the car. The surgery is only two minutes' drive away. We just need to get you there and they can sort you out.' Wrapping one of Johnny's arms around her shoulders, she hauled him to his feet with a strength she'd had no idea she possessed. His feet half-shuffled and half-dragged along the parquet floor, out into the hallway, and a million thoughts were racing through Blair's mind. They were on the opposite side of the railway crossing from the surgery. What if there was a slow moving freight train passing through and they had to wait at the crossing? Would those valuable minutes mean the difference between life and death for Johnny? She couldn't bear the thought. She was his senior officer and his welfare was in her hands. Now his life was too.

'Can't . . . breathe.'

'Come on, Johnny, just a few more steps.' Thank goodness she'd parked so close to the house. Dragging Johnny across the gravel was taking everything she had. He was leaning his full weight against her, and he barely seemed able to lift his feet up now. She pushed his body against the car and stopped him falling forward with one hand, while she opened the door with the other. Manoeuvring him onto the back seat was tricky — he didn't seem to want to move — and she had to shove him through the door and fold his legs in after him. This was no time to worry about seatbelts, or the fact that she'd banged his head on the frame of the door getting him in. If he stopped breathing, none of that was ever going to matter again.

Jumping into the front seat, she revved the engine so hard that the car screamed in protest. Yanking the gear-stick into reverse, she released the clutch and sent a spray of gravel up as the car spun in a circle and headed out onto the road. *Please don't let there be a train. Please don't let there be a train.* The mantra repeated in her head, as she sped down the lane towards the level crossing. It was clear, and if the lights started flashing now, she was still going to have to go for it. Putting her foot on the accelerator she bumped over the tracks. Half wanting to shout out and ask Johnny if he was okay, and half-terrified to do so, in case there was no response at all.

A group of people, standing outside one of the shops, turned to look at Blair's car as they raced by. Her number plate was probably being scribbled down at that very moment, but she'd happily have taken a driving ban, and the heftiest fine they could hand out, if it meant she got Johnny to the surgery in time.

She stopped the car at a ridiculous angle on the yellow lines outside the surgery doors, where there were several notices up forbidding parking, and finally turned to look at Johnny again. His eyes were half-open and his breathing was coming in gasps.

'It's alright, Johnny. We're here now, I'll get you a doctor and everything will be okay.' Fight or flight was kicking in. Blair wanted to bolt back down Balloch High Street, and keep running until she fell down. Someone else would have to deal with Johnny then, and his family, if the unthinkable happened. But she couldn't leave him. She was shouting at the top of her voice, before she even got through the surgery doors.

'I need a doctor. Now!'

'What's the matter?' The receptionist

looked terrified, as Blair ran to the desk and leant across towards her.

'My colleague's in the car, and he's had an allergic reaction. His epi-pen is missing and he can't breathe!' Blair took in a huge gulp of air. 'If you don't do something now, he'll die!'

'I'll get Noah.' The receptionist ran round the desk and along the corridor. Within seconds she was back, with Noah following on behind her, a bag in his hand.

'Is the ambulance on its way?'

'Yes, but I didn't think it could wait.' Blair was already heading back out to the car as she spoke.

'You did the right thing.' Noah's voice was immediately calming, and Blair hadn't realised how much she was shaking until he put his hand on her shoulder, as they reached the car. 'Do you know what he reacted to?'

'I know he has a nut allergy, but all he was doing was drinking a cup of tea before it happened.'

Noah examined Johnny, and turned

to Blair. 'He's definitely reacted to something, and his throat is closing up, so I don't want to wait to get him inside. I'm going to give him an injection of epinephrine. But Susie said he'd lost his epi-pen?'

'He thought it was in his coat, but . . . ' Blair couldn't believe Johnny would've lost it: it was quite literally his life line.

Noah prepared a syringe and crouched down beside where Johnny was lying, barely conscious. 'Johnny, I'm going to give you some medicine now, and it'll make it easier for you to breathe. Then we can get you back on your feet.'

'Can I do anything?' Blair was shivering, even though she wasn't cold. Watching Noah administer the injection, she'd never felt so useless in her life.

'Can you ask Susie to sort out the oxygen? If the epinephrine works as I'm hoping, we'll need to get Johnny's oxygen levels back up. He's obviously been struggling to breathe since the reaction started.'

By the time Blair was back outside, clutching the oxygen tank and mask as if *her* life depended on it, Johnny was in an upright position, slumped against the back seat. His breathing already sounded less terrifying than it had moments before.

'The epinephrine is working and Johnny's airway is more open now he's sitting up, but this should make sure he's okay until the ambulance arrives.' Noah took the oxygen tank from her and fixed the mask over Johnny's face. 'Just breathe as normally as you can; you're doing brilliantly, and the ambulance will be here any second. We need them to take you in to the hospital, just to make sure everything's okay, but I think you're through the worst.'

'Thank you.' Blair reached out and touched his arm.

'I'm just doing my job.' Noah turned to look at her again, and she suddenly understood the succession of women who'd seen her father as far more than an ordinary man, even when he'd treated them like dirt. She'd been there to take their tearful phone calls when he'd let them down and not turned up for dates, and some of them had even turned up on the doorstep virtually begging to see him. But he'd never really moved on from her mother, even if work had given him the perfect excuse to.

'Will they let me go in the ambulance with him?'

'Yes, of course, and if you want I can follow you down in my car. That way I can drive you back here if they decide to keep him in overnight. I've got one more patient to see, but I can head down after that.'

'Are you sure?' She couldn't take her eyes off Noah's hands as he repositioned the oxygen mask on Johnny's face. She'd never felt the need to lean on anyone, but right now the thought of slipping her hand into Noah's was almost overwhelming.

'It's no problem. If they decide to

release Johnny too, I can make sure he's settled at home and has all the medicines he needs.'

'I want to say thank you again, but it doesn't seem enough. Especially as I need to say sorry too.'

'Sorry for what?' Noah got up from his crouching position, as the distant wail of a siren finally pierced the air.

'For making life difficult for you during the investigation.'

'You were just doing your job, too.' Noah put a hand on her arm and she almost jumped in response. If she reached out and grabbed his hand, like the voice in her head was telling her to, she'd be the one needing an ambulance — after she collapsed with embarrassment. He'd already made it clear he was just doing his job. Mistaking his kindness for something else would have been stupid. 'If you're okay to keep speaking to Johnny, I'll brief the paramedics when they arrive and get you both on your way.'

'Of course.' Moving past him, she

crouched down beside Johnny and caught hold of his hand instead. He was going to be okay, and she was too. They'd both just had an unexpected reaction to something, but they'd both get over it. There was no other option.

* * *

It took almost two hours before Noah reached the hospital. Susie had asked if he could squeeze in one more patient in addition to the one already left on his afternoon list. It took over an hour to reach the hospital at Fort William after that, and he'd come to realise that there was no such thing as just nipping down the road in the Highlands.

Heading into the Accident and Emergency Department, he just hoped he'd be able to find out where Blair and Johnny were. She'd given him her card during the early days of the investigation into Eileen Dawson's death, so at least he had her mobile number. He doubted she'd have it switched on though, and they could almost be ready to leave if the A&E doctors had given Johnny the all clear.

To his surprise, Blair was sitting on the end of a row of fixed chairs opposite the entrance to A&E, and her face transformed when she saw him.

'I was starting to wonder if I was going to have to get the bus home.' She laughed. 'I don't know what it is about waiting in hospitals, but the time just seems to pass so slowly. Every time I look up at the clock, the hands barely seem to have moved.'

'Have you done a lot of sitting around in hospitals then?' Something about the way she'd said it suggested she had; there was almost a note of melancholy in her voice. Maybe it was related to her job — waiting around to see a victim who was undergoing treatment, or a suspect who'd been brought in with tell-tale injuries. Or maybe he'd just watched too many cop shows.

'My father's a hospital consultant

and I think I did most of my GCSE revision perched on a chair like this. No wonder my exam results didn't live up to expectations.'

'You look like you're doing pretty well to me. You're quite young for a Detective Inspector, aren't you?' He sat in the empty seat beside her.

'I suppose so.'

'That must have made your parents proud.'

'Huh.' Blair shook her head. 'Mum maybe, if she'd been around to see it, but she died when I was fifteen. And, as far as my dad is concerned, I let him down by not following him into medicine.'

'I'm sorry about your mum, but that's doctors for you. We've all got a bit of God-complex deep down.'

'You don't strike me as being like that.'

'Maybe that's because I'm happy being a GP. It sounds like your dad's much more of high flyer than me.'

'That's one description for him, but

not the one I'd necessarily use.' Blair ran a hand through her dark brown hair. 'Sorry, this is not what you came here for. You probably have to listen to this sort of thing all day — people messed up by the things their parents have said and done.'

'Most people have some sort of baggage.' Blair was the last person he'd expected to open up like this, though. It was a different side to her, but it was probably just the shock of Johnny's brush with death making her talk like this. She usually seemed pretty closed up, and she might well regret this in the morning if he didn't change the subject. 'How's Johnny doing?'

'They're running a few more tests, but he's definitely going to be okay, thanks to you.'

'You're the one who got Johnny to the surgery, and carried him out of Father Douglas' place, according to him.'

'You've seen Father Douglas?'

'Yes. He came rushing into the

surgery just after you left. Apparently, Johnny's epi-pen had fallen out of his pocket and got caught up behind some other coats when he'd hung them up. He found it after he'd called the ambulance but by the time he got down to the surgery with it, Johnny was already on his way to the hospital.'

'That sounds almost unbelievable.' Blair pulled a face. 'Did you ask him if there was any way the teacups could have come into contact with anything that might have triggered Johnny's allergy?'

'He was at a total loss about what could have caused it, and he was almost in tears when he asked if Johnny was okay.'

'The doctors here wanted to know if there was any chance he might have used almond milk in the tea. It did taste a bit weird, but I thought it was just going off. Father Douglas knows about Johnny's allergy, though. So surely he'd have realised he couldn't give him nut-based milk'

'I would have thought so, unless he just didn't join the dots. But Father Douglas seems too traditional to me to go in for something like that anyway.' Being suspicious might have been an occupational hazard for Blair, but surely she didn't really think Father Douglas had planned all this? What could possibly be in it for him? Even if Noah stretched the bounds of his imagination as far as it would go — and considered that the priest was capable of killing Eileen and Fraser — Father Douglas attempting to kill Johnny would just make things worse for him, plus ensure he became the number one suspect for the murders. It was just too unlikely.

'I'm sure we had normal milk at his place the first time; I'd have noticed that weird taste otherwise. And I just don't see him being involved in the murders.' There were dark shadows under Blair's eyes. 'But I shouldn't be talking to you about any of this.'

'Because I'm still a suspect?'

'No, but you're not Johnny, so I can't use you as a sounding board, or risk having you talking to anyone else about it.'

'I wouldn't do that.'

'I know.' She smiled, and for a moment he wished he was Johnny. Not because he wanted to be lying in a hospital bed recovering from a life-threatening anaphylactic shock, but because then he'd get to spend all day talking to Blair. And right now, that was far more appealing than it should have been.

'Maybe we should talk about something a bit safer.' She smiled again. 'So do you like it here, in Scotland I mean? Or are you missing the buzz of London?'

'I love it here. It was my wife's favourite place, too. She painted landscapes and even though she lived in central London, she always seemed to want to paint the wilds of Scotland more than anywhere else.'

'It must be really hard, being here

without her.' The tell-tale tilt of Blair's head threw him off course. She felt sorry for him, and he didn't want the lie to sit between them, especially after she'd opened up to him about her father. He was going to have to tell her the truth.

'I do miss Katie, but we were never a conventional couple. She was my best friend's little sister, and a close friend in her own right even though she was quite a bit younger than me and Andrew. But we'd never have got married if she hadn't been ill.'

'You don't have to talk about this, if it's difficult for you.'

'It's okay, there aren't many people I can talk to about it.' There was no one. Not even his own parents knew the truth about him and Katie. 'She had leukaemia, but she didn't respond to treatment in the way everyone hoped she would. Her doctors had put her on another round of experimental treatment, but they'd been honest with her about the low likelihood of it working.'

'That must have been awful.'

'It was, and she was devastated. I saw her one weekend at her brother's place. She was heartbroken about all the things she was going to miss out on, and most of all that she'd never know what it felt like to fall in love and get married. We'd gone out a few times a couple of years before she was diagnosed, but I didn't think it had been anything serious. We'd always been friends, and I thought we were on the same page about it being better to keep it that way. But there she was, sitting in front of me, saying that I was the closest she'd come to finding her soul mate, and that she wished things had worked out differently.'

'And that made you realise you had feelings for her too?' Blair's voice was warm, and so different to the way she'd spoken to him in the past, her professional persona left behind.

'It's when I realised I loved her, but not in the way she was talking about. She was like a little sister to me, and I wanted to do whatever I could to make her last few months everything she wanted them to be.' Noah let go of a long breath, not sure if what he was about to say would make him sound like a complete fraud or not. But he certainly felt like one. 'I sat there and held her in my arms, and she told me she loved me, that she had since we'd been kids, and that she'd been heart-broken when the few dates we'd had didn't turn into anything else. She started crying again, saying that no one would ever love her now, and the words were out of my mouth before I could stop them. I told her I loved her too, and that I wished I could turn back time. It was true, in a way. I did love her, but I was never *in love* with her. And I really did want to turn back time, to before she was ill, so that she'd have the chance to experience it all for real.'

'What you did was amazing.' Blair squeezed his hand. 'You gave Katie what she wanted the most.'

'But it wasn't true. I knew she

wanted to get married more than anything, so I planned the most romantic proposal I could think of. I went completely over the top, and booked out the aquarium. She'd loved scuba diving before she got too ill to do it, and I'd quite often take her there to walk under the glass tunnels, where she could pretend she was still lost in that world. One day, I arranged for a diver to be in one of the tanks, holding up a sign asking Katie to marry me. I got down on one knee, and presented her with a ring — the whole works. But I could never tell her the truth, and now I feel like the biggest jerk in the world.'

'My mum said to me once that love comes in many different guises.' Blair's eyes were glassy, and for a moment he was tempted to put his arm around her to comfort her. But he'd have been lying again if he did, this time to himself, about the real reason he wanted to do it. 'I think she was trying to make me feel better because Dad had blown up at me about something again, and she said he was only so controlling because he loved me, and wanted the best for me. I don't know if that's true, but I do know that what you did would have made Katie *feel* loved. And just because what you felt for her wasn't romantic love, it doesn't make it any less real.'

'It really seemed like the right thing to do at the time, and she told me she was the happiest she'd ever been on our wedding day. We managed a few days in Scotland for our honeymoon because she was too ill to fly, and we came up by train. There was never anything physical between us because she was far too unwell, so at least I didn't have to take the lie that far. She'd always wanted to go to Loch Ness, and we managed a few touristy things, but her health deteriorated quickly after that, and she told the doctors that she didn't want to go through another round of treatment. We all just concentrated on making as many of her dreams come true as we could, and keeping her as pain free as possible. I couldn't even tell my best friend the truth about me and Katie because he was her brother. And after she died, I couldn't stand the sympathy that everyone was directing at me, because I didn't deserve it. That's when I decided to move up here.'

'Do you think Katie made the right decision about stopping the treatment?'

'As a doctor, it was hard for me not to try to persuade her to use every option she had before giving up. But as someone who cared about her, I could tell she'd had enough. So I supported her decision.' He looked directly at Blair. 'But I didn't do anything to help her along, if that's what you're wondering. Although if she'd been in a lot of pain at the end, I'm not sure what I would have done.'

'I've never thought you had anything to do with Katie's death.'

'But you *did* think I might have murdered a patient?' He couldn't help laughing at the look on her face.

'I'm not sure I ever really believed

that, either. But I wouldn't have been doing my job if I hadn't followed up every possibility.'

'And you're very good at it.'

Blair sighed. 'If I was that good at it, I'd know who was responsible for both deaths by now. Instead, my Detective Constable is in hospital and I'm about to hand over the case with only a series of dead ends to show for it.'

'It's not over until it's over.'

'Unless Father Douglas does turn out to be the criminal mastermind behind all of this, then I think it's over for my team already.'

'This is going to sound really weird, given how we met, but I'm actually going to miss seeing you.' It was a weight off his shoulders not to be under suspicion any more, but the thought of never seeing Blair again definitely took some of the shine off it.

'You're right, it is weird!' It was her turn to laugh. 'But I do know what you mean.'

'Blair Hannah?' A nurse called out

her name, and she stood up. 'You can come through and see your friend now.'

'Are you sure you don't mind waiting?' Blair turned to Noah, and he nodded in response. 'Thank you, hopefully I won't be long. See you in a bit.'

She disappeared through the double doors with the nurse, and he picked up a discarded newspaper from another chair. He was just doing his bit, he'd have waited at the hospital for anyone in the same circumstances. But if he tried to convince himself that Blair was just anyone, then the lies he'd told himself would just keep stacking up.

8

Noah slipped his mobile phone back into his desk drawer, as the next patient knocked on the door. Blair's message had thanked him again for waiting for her at the hospital, and she'd also given him an update on Johnny's progress. They'd released him from hospital after a night's observation, and the doctors were as certain as possible that the allergic reaction had been triggered by almond milk. Although Father Douglas was still insisting he'd never even tried it, let alone had it in his kitchen.

Noah had come to Balloch Pass for a simpler life, but it was turning out to be anything but that, especially since he couldn't deny how much he enjoyed Blair's company. He hadn't felt like that about anyone since before Katie's illness. Guilt had turned his feelings off, but they'd come flooding back at the hospital, like a river bursting its banks. Maybe he was just confusing the unburdening of his problems with something else, but he'd certainly slept better since he'd told Blair the truth.

'Come in.' Noah responded to the knock on his consulting room door, and a young man in a hooded jumper walked in. 'Hello, Brendan isn't it? What can I do for you today?'

'I think I've got shingles.' Brendan grimaced. 'I've got a nasty sort of rash on my back, that's got blistered. I had chicken pox as a bairn and when my girlfriend took a picture of it on her phone, it looks exactly like the pictures online.'

'Shingles can be very painful. Let's have a look at you, and we can see if your girlfriend should be after my job.' Noah smiled. He didn't mind patients coming to him with a diagnosis in mind, as long as they didn't get too fixated on it, or worry themselves half to death with what they'd read. As soon as Brendan lifted up his top, Noah could see that his girlfriend had been spot on. 'You're absolutely right, it's shingles. Has it been very painful?'

'Aye, I can't even bear to put a tee-shirt on, they're too tight. So, I've been living in hoodies.'

'Are you in pain now?'

'A bit, but I'm worried about Holly, my girlfriend.' Brendan bit his lip. 'She's about five weeks pregnant. I told her this probably wasn't shingles, even though I knew it was, because she's terrified it might affect the baby. We've been trying for nearly a year now and she'll kill me if anything goes wrong.'

'Has she had chicken pox, do you know?'

'Aye, she said she has, but she's never had shingles. I should have stayed away from her as soon as I noticed the rash, but I didn't realise what it was.'

'Don't worry.' Noah typed a web address into his computer. 'If your girlfriend has had chicken pox, then you can't pass the shingles virus on to her, you can only give her chicken pox if she hasn't already had it. I'll print this information off for you and you can reassure her there's nothing to worry about.'

'Oh thank heavens for that, you've no idea how relieved I am.' Brendan's face said a lot more than he realised. It was good to have the sort of consultation where Noah could sort out the problem, and ease his patient's concerns at the same time.

'What do you do for a living, Brendan? If you're in contact with the public, it might be best for you to stay off work until the blisters start to dry up; that way there's no risk of you giving chicken pox to someone who hasn't had it.'

'I'm a personal trainer, but I've had to cancel my gym sessions anyway, because I was in too much pain.'

'Let's get that sorted for you then. I'll prescribe some acyclovir, which is an anti-viral medication, and amitriptyline for the pain. The shingles virus can damage the nerve endings and that's what causes the pain. There's a chance it might carry on, even after the rash completely clears up, but you can come back to the surgery if that turns out to be the case.'

'Thanks Doctor. I'll ask for an appointment with you, if I need to come back in. I'd prefer to see you again, if that's okay?'

'Of course.' Noah handed over the prescription, and the printed information sheet. It had been a while since anyone had said that to him, and things were definitely changing for the better since he'd been taken off Blair's suspect list. He had a hunch she'd made sure people found that out, and he wanted the chance to thank her. As it turned out, the opportunity came much more quickly than he expected.

* * *

Blair closed her eyes, mentally going over the evidence they'd collected so far, and trying to make sense of the vital clue they must have been missing. A knock on her office door broke her train of thought.

'Come in.'

'Sorry, Boss.' Chrissie stepped inside the office. 'I know we're due to have a final briefing later, before we hand the case over next week, but some of the results have come back on the typewriter.'

'Anything that might be a game changer?'

'None of the prints match Colin Hendry's, or anyone else's on the database.' Chrissie shrugged her shoulders. 'But they've started ribbon analysis, and evaluation of the imprints made by the keys. They aren't hopeful of being able to lift enough off the ribbon to match it to a particular owner, but the letter was definitely written on that machine.'

'How can they tell that?'

'Apparently they compare the individual defects on the machine, with any identifying issues in the typeface on the document. And there's only something like a one in a million chance it could have been produced on any other machine.'

'So Colin could have typed the will on it, and just wiped his fingerprints off.'

'There were lots of finger prints on the machine, just none they could identify. And definitely not his.' Chrissie sighed. 'I suppose he could have typed the will wearing a pair of latex gloves.'

'It's a possibility. But you don't think it was him, do you?'

Chrissie was already shaking her head. 'No, Boss, I don't, but neither do you, do you?'

'No, I don't.' She never had. Colin had a water tight alibi for Fraser Daniels' death, and Eileen had been like a second mum to him. The only common element was Father Douglas and, as ridiculous as that seemed, they were running out of options. 'Do you know if we have Father Douglas' fingerprints on file?'

'He's never actually been into the station, as far as I know.'

'We'd better check that out then, so we can eliminate him from our inquiries.'

'What about Dr Bradshaw?'

'He gave his fingerprints voluntarily when he was first interviewed.' She hadn't been able to get Noah out of her head since that night at the hospital. When he'd opened up about what had happened with his wife, she'd seen a whole new side to him. He obviously carried some guilt about what he'd let Katie believe, but he shouldn't. He'd done absolutely the right thing, and it was more obvious than ever what sort of person he really was.

Blair wasn't even sure any more whether Eileen's will *had* been altered by someone else. As much as her family seemed convinced, it was the fact they had the Superintendent's ear that had resulted in such an in-depth investigation in the beginning. Both Noah and Father Douglas did a lot for the community, and sometimes people just wanted to reward that. The Procurator

Fiscal had ordered a second autopsy on Eileen Dawson, but her murder might have nothing to do with the changes in her will.

'Is there anything else you want me to do?' Chrissie took a step towards the door.

'No, I'm just going through all the evidence in case there's something obvious we've missed. I think we've explored all the connections between Eileen Dawson and Fraser Daniels, but I'm looking again at the other recent unexpected deaths to see if there's something we've missed.' Blair's eyes were already stinging. But it was like losing something that you've searched everywhere for — you just can't stop looking, even when it's time to accept you should give up.

'I'll let you know when I've spoken to Father Douglas, Boss, but give me a shout if there's anything you need.'

'Thanks, Chrissie.' What she needed was to find the missing piece of the jigsaw before they handed over the case, and to get Noah Bradshaw out of her head. But not necessarily in that order.

* * *

'That was so good.' Evie pushed her plate away and rested a hand on the top of her baby bump. 'I can't get enough of spicy food at the moment, and junior here seems to approve. It feels like the baby's turning cartwheels tonight, although I think it's getting a bit tight on space.'

'Since most people seem to believe eating spicy food can bring on labour, are you surprised at the baby's reaction, darling?' Alasdair took hold of his wife's hand, and Noah caught the look they exchanged. Had he and Katie looked like that from the outside? He hoped that she'd believed it as much as she'd seemed to, but there was an atmosphere around Evie and Alasdair that no one could fake. Maybe it was because the baby, which would complete their family, was only weeks away from arriving. But, whatever it was, Noah wanted to find it one day. He'd never believed in all that stuff about soul mates and *the one* — he was a scientist at heart — but he believed in chemistry, and there'd been enough of that between him and Blair to make him open up to her. He'd told her things he'd never told anyone.

'You can't deny me a curry. It's a Balloch Pass Inn speciality, and this could be our last night out for a long time.' Evie grinned. 'Susie might be willing to babysit for Bronte and Rory, but I'm not sure how she'd feel about taking on a newborn as well.'

'Tonight is my treat.' Noah shook his head when his friends started to protest. 'It's to thank you for standing by me, and believing in me when the police were investigating Eileen's death.'

'We never had any doubt.' Alasdair said, as Evie nodded in agreement. 'And we're the ones who should be buying you dinner. We're just so glad you'll be staying on now, and that you're willing to support the locum after the baby arrives, while we work out how we're going to spread the hours between us, once we're a family of five.'

'If someone had told me three years ago that I'd have three children, I'd never have believed them.' Evie exchanged another look with Alasdair. 'But I thank God every day that I ended up in Balloch Pass by whatever twist of fate it was that brought me here.'

'Do you think that's what it was? Fate?' Noah didn't believe in that either.

'I can't explain it any other way.' Evie tapped the side of her nose. 'And after all you've been through, fate will find a way of bringing you what you need, too.'

'After being implicated in a murder, all I want is a quiet life!' Noah raised his glass, hoping that would be enough. But he'd lied to a dying woman and, if fate had any sense of justice, he'd be paying for that for the rest of his life.

* * *

Fresh air would clear Blair's head. The words in the evidence file had started to swim, and even making the text bigger on the computer screen hadn't helped. She needed a break. The rest of the team had already gone home, and it was time she headed off too, but she just couldn't seem to accept this was it. Someone else was going to find out what had really happened to Eileen and Fraser, and it would be no thanks to her.

Maybe she was losing her touch, or maybe she'd never really had it when she'd been down at the Met. Had she been carried by colleagues, with more talent in their little fingers than she'd ever have? Being in a small team, like the one she headed up now, could expose that and she felt every inch the failure she was.

'Ah, so you are still alive. Is there a reason you haven't returned any of my calls?' Her father moved out of the shadows, at the bottom of the steps outside the police station. Some detective she was. A serial killer could have been lurking there, ready to slit her throat, and she wouldn't have seen him until it was too late. Finding her father standing there was only slightly preferable.

'I've been busy with the case.' She was already trying to turn away from him, fighting the desire to run back up the steps to the safety of her office, where he'd need a security pass, so he wouldn't be able to get to her. At least not physically.

'I hear it hasn't gone too well and that you'll be handing it over soon?' There was that familiar look of disdain.

'How do you know about the case?'

'Just someone at the club.' She'd known the answer before he'd even responded. It had been a mistake to come back to Scotland, and settle so close to her father.

'We've gathered a lot of useful evidence.'

‘But you didn’t solve the case.’

‘Do you cure every patient you operate on?’ She almost spat the words out, pressing her nails into her palm. He was winning again, getting to her, just like he wanted.

‘It’s not the same thing and you know it. Some of what I do is in the hands of God.’

‘Oh, and there was me thinking that’s who you see when you look in the mirror.’

‘I didn’t come here for you to take your failures out on me. I thought you might have moved on by now, Blair.’ His voice was level, but his mouth was set in a grim line. He wasn’t the only one who could hit a nerve.

‘What exactly did you come here for then?’

‘To see if you’d come to your senses yet, about throwing away the chance of a half-decent career with the Met. I might never believe that police work is stretching you to your full potential, but hiding out here, in this little backwater

. . . Let's face it; you're never going to get any better at the job if you don't challenge yourself. If you surround yourself with mediocrity, what else do you expect?'

'I don't expect anything anymore. Least of all from you.' Shaking, she headed back up the steps. He was never going to change, but neither was she, and that was something that terrified her — the possibility she might be more like him than she could bear.

* * *

Noah had planned to leave the pub straight after Evie and Alasdair headed home. But he'd been cornered by Angus McTavish, an elderly farmer who lived on the outskirts of Balloch Pass, and who wanted Noah's opinion on a mole that had appeared on his left earlobe. After he'd reassured Angus that it was nothing to worry about, the old man had insisted on buying him a drink, and so he'd still been at the bar when Blair walked in.

'Are you following me?' He smiled as she came and stood next to him. He'd used the same line he had when they'd met in the market place, but that seemed a lifetime ago now.

'Not anymore.' She raised her eyebrows and it was hard to tell if she was joking, but he liked the curve of her mouth when something was making her smile. She should do it more often.

'So, who are you following tonight and, more to the point, can I get you a drink whilst you're waiting for them to show up?'

'I'm not following anyone, I was just hoping that someone might want to come and speak to me about the case if I hung out here for a bit. I just need the right lead and all this could be sorted before the other team take over. But a drink would be good, if I'm not keeping you from anything?' She looked around as she spoke, but Angus had moved to the other end of the bar and he was chatting to another group of locals.

'No, I had dinner with Evie and Alasdair, but they had to get back for the baby sitter.' Noah signalled to the barman. 'What can I get you?'

'I'm not on duty, and a gin and tonic would go down well after the day I've had.'

'Coming right up.' Noah turned to her and smiled. It was a long time since he'd done this — had a drink in a bar with someone who wasn't a friend, or a colleague. 'If you want to grab that table in the corner, I'll bring it over, as soon as the barman finally manages to get over here.'

When Noah got to the table, Blair took the gin and tonic and drained half the glass before he sat down. 'Sorry, but it's been a hell of a day.'

'Anything you want to talk about?'

'Maybe after a few more of these.' She swirled the liquid around the glass. 'Although I don't usually drink, so one might turn out to be enough.'

'How's Johnny?'

'He's good, and he wanted to come

straight back to work, but I've told him he's got to have a few days off. Johnny coming home from the hospital is the one good thing to happen this week.' Blair drained the rest of her drink. 'I'll get us another, and you can tell me something that will cheer me up. You must have loads of funny stories about people with objects stuck in weird places.'

She headed back to the bar before he could respond. He didn't really want another drink, but he wanted to spend more time with Blair — the mask she wore was slipping, and he wanted the chance to see her for who she really was.

He looked at her back view, as she stood at the bar. She was tall and slim, with long dark hair, and the barman leapt into action as soon as he saw her. Her frustration at not being able to solve the case was tangible, but there was something else bothering her. He'd thought it might be to do with Johnny until she'd said that he was okay.

'Here you go. I got us another couple of drinks each, so we don't have to keep going up to the bar. I hope you're not working tomorrow.'

'I've got the weekend off, what about you?'

'The way things are going, I might end up with my whole life off. I can't get any further with this case and I'm going to have to hand it over with no firm leads. It's nothing like the detective shows on TV. It's frustrating and exhausting, and there are hardly ever any good car chases!' She laughed, but she was gripping her glass so tightly her knuckles had turned white.

'So the Major Investigation Team are taking over, now you know it's definitely murder?' A look of surprise crossed her face, as he spoke. 'I did a bit of research when I thought I might end up being investigated by them.'

'I'm really sorry about that.' She squeezed his hand briefly. It was a mystery to him why she didn't have someone else to confide in, or talk to about her rubbish week. She was beautiful, and obviously good at her job, despite her frustration at not being able to solve the murders in Balloch Pass.

'I know it wasn't personal.' His hand felt colder as soon as she moved hers away. 'So is that why it's been such a bad week. Having to hand the case over?'

'That would have been bad enough. Even without my dad, who seems to get the inside track on every investigation I'm involved in, showing up at work and telling me just what a disappointment I am to him. As if I could have forgotten the hundred or so times he's already told me that.'

'I thought your dad was a hospital consultant? Does he work with the police too?' It could be tough working in the same field as one of your parents; there would be always comparisons, and more often than not an unhealthy dose of competition. Noah's sister had followed their parents into the law, and all three were practising barristers in the Temple area of London. The closest Noah had come was working as a barista in a coffee chain whilst he'd been at university. He'd seen his sister and parents butt heads far too many times, not helped by the fact that they all argued for a living. So he could understand the tensions it might cause if Blair's father did work for the same force as her.

'Oh, no, he'd never do that. He wouldn't ever give up his hospital work to get involved with anything I do. He couldn't look down on my job any more than he does, if he made it his full time occupation to do so. He just knows people in high places *every-where*, and the police force is no different.' Blair sighed. 'It doesn't do much for your self-esteem, to know that your dad and one of your commanding officers have been discussing what a big fat failure you are.'

'Did he really say that?'

'Not quite, but he was happy to

remind me that I hadn't solved the case. I already felt bad enough; there was really no need to remind me.' She took another drink. 'He also told me, yet again, that I've thrown away my only chance of having a worthwhile career in the police by leaving the Met.'

'You must know that's not true. I can see how Johnny looks up to you, and I trusted you, even when you were questioning me about Eileen Dawson's death.'

'I might finally have found out the truth about you, but I'm not sure Eileen's family would share your sentiment. Whoever killed their mother is still out there, and now Fraser is gone too. If I'd been better at my job, he might still be alive.'

'I'm guessing the police force is like the NHS, and resources are more stretched than they've ever been?' She nodded as he spoke. 'In which case you've done brilliantly so far, but you can only follow so many lines of inquiry with the resources you've got. Maybe your dad touched on a nerve. If what he said makes you feel so bad, could he be right about your decision to leave the Met? Are you missing it?'

'Not really, but what I do miss is the distance from my father, and the fact that he didn't belong to the same clubs as any of my senior officers. There was none of this feeling of being judged because I'm his daughter — either by him or any of his cronies from the club. If anything made me go back to London, it would be that.'

'What made you come home to Scotland in the first place?' He still wanted to get past the surface with Blair, and she seemed grateful of the chance to talk.

'My counsellor.' She laughed again, but it was a hollow, joyless sound. 'I'm sorry, you probably don't want to hear all of this, and I should have stuck to the orange juice. Gin always turns me into a cry baby.'

'I do want to hear it, but only if you want to tell me. I went on for long enough about what happened between me and Katie, the least I can do is to repay the favour. Maybe we should start a support group for escapees from London, who've packed up all their issues and brought them along to Scotland?' He grinned, and this time she looked like she meant it when she returned his smile.

'My counsellor would probably approve of that! He told me to come back to Scotland to sort out my problems with Dad.' She shrugged. 'As you can see, it's going really well.'

'Have things always been like this between you, or is it just since you lost your mum?'

'Dad always thought he knew best, but she used to rein him in a bit and balance things out. He got worse than ever after she died, and there was no one to take the pressure off, or tell me I wasn't doing so badly after all.'

'All that matters in the end, you know, is what you think of yourself.'

'Now you sound like my counsellor!'

'Guilty as charged, although I've only done a couple of levels of training.' Noah picked up his drink. 'Sorry if it sounds like I'm talking rubbish.'

'No, I know you're right, and the twenty or so self-help books I've read say the same thing — that I need to stand up to him, and tell him the only person's approval I need is my own. I almost managed it today, but I can't keep my emotions in check when I'm around him. He's always been able to press my buttons. I know in his own twisted way that he loves me, but he just has a funny way of showing it.' She pushed up the sleeve of her jumper. 'This is what he did when he caught me with a packet of cigarettes in my school bag at sixteen.'

There was a small round scar on her arm. 'Is that a cigarette burn?'

'Yeah, some parents make their kids smoke the whole packet, when they find them with cigarettes. But there was only one cigarette left in the pack, so he lit it and then stubbed it out on my arm.'

Pushing her sleeve back down, Blair wiped her eyes with the back of her hand. 'When I cried, he told me he was doing it for my own good, and that if I thought the burn was painful, I should see some of the cancer patients he dealt with in the oncology clinics.'

'Oh Blair, I don't really know what to say.' It was true, but when she put her hand on his again and squeezed it, he knew what he wanted to *do*. He wanted to hold her, and take the bad stuff away. He'd felt the same about Katie, but this was different. He'd felt sorry for Katie, but there was more to it than that with Blair, and that just made things worse. Katie had died believing everything he'd said to her, and all Blair wanted was a listening ear. What went through his head when he looked at Blair betrayed both women.

'You don't have to say anything.' Blair's voice was soft. 'I just needed to get it off my chest, and I'm glad you were here.'

'Me too.' Blair Hannah was something special, and in another life he might have told her. But all she wanted was a friend, and he had to honour Katie's memory. He had no choice.

* * *

'Thanks for this.' Blair put three sugars in her coffee. She usually preferred tea, but sometimes only the bitter, shake-you-awake, taste of strong coffee would do the job. Noah had switched from ordering gin to coffee about three drinks in. And if she was going to make it home in one piece, it was a good job he had. Her father had always hated drinking — almost as much as he hated smoking — which was the main reason she'd done both.

'It's just a coffee.' Noah laughed, and part of her wished he'd kept ordering the drinks. It might have knocked the edge off both their inhibitions, and she might have found out what it was like to kiss him. She'd accidentally caught the end of a celebrity dating show the week before, when she'd come in late from a stint of unpaid overtime. There'd been a so-called flirting expert on the show, giving advice about how to move in for a kiss — the upside triangle they'd called it. You had to look from the left eye, to the right, down to the mouth and then up again. If the other person moved in for a kiss, then you were doing it right. She found herself trying it out on Noah — just in the name of experimentation of course — but all she'd got in return was a funny look.

'Are you okay? Have I got something on my face?' Noah was still looking puzzled.

'No, sorry, I was just thinking.' Thank goodness she wasn't really trying to flirt with him — she was obviously beyond help. Maybe that's what came from putting work before everything else for so long.

'Do you ever switch off? I can almost see the cogs whirring in your brain.

You're still thinking about the evidence, aren't you?'

'Something like that.' She stared down into the blackness of the coffee, it was easier than looking at him.

'I think you just need a good night's sleep if you can get one, to put this all into perspective. I asked Maggie, the landlady, to order you a cab home before closing time. I hope you don't think I'm trying to run your life, too, but I thought it might be difficult to get one right out here otherwise.'

'Of course I don't mind, and it was silly of me not to sort one out. I still think that it's like London, and you can just walk outside and hail a taxi at any time, or get an uber on your phone.'

'Angus McTavish would probably have given you a lift home in the back of his tractor, but he might have wanted a second opinion on his current medical condition, and I couldn't in all conscience put you through that.'

'I think we interviewed him after Fraser Daniels died. He had some interesting theories about a hotel chain wanting to buy up land in Balloch Pass, and getting rid of Fraser because he refused to sell.' She put another sugar in her coffee. 'But there was absolutely no evidence to support the theory.'

'He told me once he knew for a fact that the moon landings were a big hoax, so you should probably take everything he says with a pinch of salt.'

'Do you believe everything you see, then?' She found her eyes drawn to his mouth again, but forced them back up to meet his gaze as he shook his head.

'No, I like to form my own opinions, but some things are undeniable.' He tilted his head forward slightly, and she couldn't seem to stop herself mirroring it, until their faces were much closer than would normally have been comfortable.

'Noah, the taxi you ordered is here!' The landlady shouted out from her position behind the bar, and Blair's head jerked back, the spell broken.

'I'll walk you out.'

'You don't need to do that.' But he was already standing up as she spoke. 'Thank you, though.'

The sky outside the pub was almost violet, bathed in the light of a full moon and a blanket of stars. If she'd been looking for a romantic moment, then this was it. Turning towards him, to say goodbye, as they drew level with the taxi, her heel caught in the grate above the pub cellar and sent her sprawling towards him.

'I've got you.' Taking hold of her arms, he steadied her, and this time she didn't stop to think about flirting techniques. Something else took over as she pressed her mouth against his. For a moment he seemed to hesitate, but then he kissed her back.

'If you two are going to spend all night canoodling, then I better set the meter running.' The taxi driver, who must have been seventy if he was a day, leered out of the rolled-down window of his cab. And Noah pulled away, moving to open the back door of the car, as if he couldn't wait to get rid of her.

'Get a good night's sleep but drink plenty of water first, and you should have a clear head in the morning.' He closed the door as soon as she got in the back of the taxi, before she had the chance to answer. Seeing things more clearly in the morning was all well and good. But the way she'd lunged towards him, and then been shoved into the back of the taxi like an uninvited guest at a party, was something she'd sooner forget.

9

Blair took a taxi to her meeting with the head of the Major Investigation Team, who were finally taking over the case. He thanked Blair for the work her team had done and gave permission for Bill and Chrissie to finalise the inquiries they were working on in the community. But she could read between the lines; the case was no closer to being solved than it had been when her team were asked to look into the concerns of Eileen's family. Next time they probably wouldn't be trusted with anything more serious than following up a spate of unpaid parking tickets, and wouldn't her father just love that.

She wasn't even supposed to be working. So after the meeting, she phoned Bill to let him know that he and Chrissie could carry on with what they were doing, and that she would be taking the rest of the day, and the next day, off. She'd insisted that Johnny took the remainder of the week off, and he'd phoned to say that Vicky, the community police constable he'd started dating just before he'd ended up in hospital, was taking very good care of him. Blair was happy for him, but it was another reminder that she was failing on all counts.

She wanted to stick her head under a pillow for the next two days when she thought about kissing Noah. He'd seemed into it for about half a minute, but then he hadn't been able to bundle her into the taxi quickly enough. If she hadn't had to pick her car up from Balloch Pass, she'd happily never have gone there again. The thought of bumping into Noah Bradshaw made her stomach churn. She'd gone from accusing him of murder to throwing herself at him, and she wasn't sure if he'd preferred being cross-examined to being kissed.

The taxi driver dropped her off in

the square outside the Balloch Pass Inn, her phone buzzing as she stepped out of the car. It was an email letting her know that the Major Investigation Team would be looking into the deaths of another two patients who'd died unexpectedly. Forwarding the email on to Bill, she added a quick line to ask whether he or Chrissie had collected any intelligence on either of the potential victims. At this stage, she could use any brownie points she could get. It was still difficult to believe there might be a serial killer in a town like Balloch Pass — somewhere she might have liked to call home under different circumstances. She was still renting a flat, but she had planned to buy somewhere in the area. There was beautiful countryside surrounding the town, but enough services to get by without having to drive miles to the next big town to go shopping, eat out, or even see a doctor. But she wouldn't be staying. Her dad was right, her shortfalls were all too obvious in a small team like the one she was heading up. She was going to request a transfer back to the Met, and the anonymity of life in a big city, where her father wouldn't be able to find out anything about her work or her personal life. Except in the unlikely scenario of her deciding to tell him.

'How are you feeling this morning?' The voice was instantly recognisable, and it belonged to the last person she wanted to see.

'I'm fine, thanks. You?' Pretending she hadn't seen him wasn't an option.

'Look, about last night . . . ' She'd opened her mouth to stop him when her phone started to ring. Silently thanking whoever it was for interrupting her conversation with Noah, she held up her hand. She didn't even care if it was her father; for once speaking even to him would have been a blessed relief.

'Sorry, I'm going to have to take this.' Turning away from him, she didn't even bother to check the caller display.

With any luck Noah would be gone by the time she finished the call. 'Hello?'

'Boss, it's Bill. I got your email and those two names you forwarded on to me rang a bell. I looked through the file, and we had copies of their death certificates from when we were looking into the crematorium records.'

'Right, and is there anything on the certificates that might be useful to pass on to the Major Investigation Team?' Blair kept her voice as low as she could, but she could sense Noah still standing behind her.

'Not really. They were both recorded as heart attacks after the pathology reports, from what I can see in the files, but that fits with what Eileen Dawson's death looked like initially.'

'So there's nothing worth noting from the information you've collected?'

'Only that one death was notified by Dr Evie James, and the other by her husband. So unless all three doctors were in it, or Noah Bradshaw was able to fool the other two, I think that finally lays the idea that he had anything to do with it to rest for good.' Bill sounded almost disappointed. 'And he isn't the first doctor a patient has left money to, is he? Just as well her son-in-law is mates with the Superintendent, or all this might have been written off. I suppose sometimes nepotism pays off.'

'I suppose it does. *Sometimes*.' And sometimes those sort of relationships caused big problems. 'I might see if I can speak to Alasdair and Evie James, whilst I'm here, just to see if there's anything useful they can recall.'

'I thought you had the afternoon off, Boss?'

'I do, but you know me, Bill.'

'Aye, I do, Boss. But you get some rest tomorrow if you can, and go and do something fun. It's been a tough few weeks.'

'Thanks, I will.' She'd miss Bill and the others when she went back to London, but it was for the best.

'Is there a new development in the case?' Noah asked, as she turned around to face him. Part of her wanted to tell him that it was none of his business. If he wasn't interested in her, then he didn't have the right to be interested in anything about her — not even the case he'd been implicated in. But the truth was that she needed him. He'd know where Evie and Alasdair were, and he might have some information on the patients who'd died too. Speaking to all three doctors was the best chance of obtaining some information that might actually be useful, so she'd have to get him on side, however awkward that felt.

'The new team looking into Fraser and Eileen's deaths are going to extend the investigation to look in more depth at a couple of other patients who died unexpectedly.' She opened the email on her phone. 'Tim Kennedy and Emily Ferguson both died of suspected heart attacks, even though neither of them were known to have a pre-existing heart condition, and they were both relatively young.'

'And you think Evie and Alasdair might know something about it?' Noah narrowed his eyes.

'Don't look at me like that.' Blair put her phone back into her pocket. 'I'm not accusing them of being involved in the patients' deaths, like the three of you are in some big plot to wipe out half the population of Balloch Pass. It's just that they were the attending doctors who verified the deaths, and I thought they might have a bit more insight into the patients' general health at the time of their deaths. The Major Investigation Team will go through their medical records, but a bit of inside information might help speed things up.'

'Evie is working her last shift at the surgery today, before she goes on maternity leave, so they should both be finishing work at about half five. I know they haven't got the kids tonight as their uncle is over for a visit, and he's picking them up from school and taking them to an adventure park in Aviemore for the weekend. That will be a good time to speak to them, if you can hang around until then?'

'Okay.' It was three thirty. She could kill two hours in Balloch Pass, maybe she'd even go for a walk in the woodland at Coille Water, and get some of that relaxation Bill had been banging on about.

'I'm not working this afternoon, if you fancy a drink?'

'I think last night was enough, don't you? And I've got to drive later.' Blair's scalp was prickling again. Spending two hours making small talk with a man that she was so blatantly attracted to — when he so obviously wasn't attracted to her — was about as appealing as spending the next two hours pulling her eyelashes out one by one.

'I just meant a cup of tea or coffee; there's a nice little tearoom just up the road, called Lovetts. Have you tried it? It's opposite the cottage I'm renting from Alasdair and Evie.'

'Right.' She'd been about to say a

simple 'no thanks', but curiosity got the better of her. She wanted to know where he lived — not in a stalker-ish sort of way — it was just the detective in her. She was interested to find out if it lived up to her expectations. That was all. But why he wanted to spend two hours with her was another mystery. He'd virtually slammed the taxi door shut on her yesterday, but here he was inviting her for round two. Maybe he liked having women throwing themselves at him, just so he could reject them. But that didn't sit with the way he'd treated Katie and what he'd done to make sure she felt loved. It didn't fit with what Blair had learnt about him over the time she'd known him, either. As much as she wanted to think otherwise right now, Noah Bradshaw was a good man.

* * *

They'd talked about everything and nothing for the first forty-five minutes.

Noah had been tempted to launch into an explanation about the night before as soon as he'd seen Blair. He could have told her he'd been up half the night thinking about what it had been like to finally kiss her, and that putting her in the taxi home had been all about self-preservation. But he didn't, he couldn't risk what he felt for Blair deepening into something he'd never had for his wife. What would Katie think if she knew that kissing Blair made him forget everything else, even her? And what would Andrew and the rest of her family think, if they knew? They were all still grieving for Katie, and Noah falling for someone else so quickly would have made it seem as though she'd never meant that much to him. But she had, just not in the way they'd all wanted to believe. No one had raised an eyebrow at the pace of their romance, and how it had aligned itself to Katie's illness, or questioned whether it was for real. They'd all just wanted Katie's dreams to come true, and he couldn't risk tainting it, even now.

'So what will happen when you've completely handed this case over?' Noah was running out of small talk, but years of friendship with Andrew had taught him that a copper was always willing to talk about work. Maybe not the details, but, like doctors, the best ones lived and breathed what they did. It was in their bones, like the writing printed through a stick of rock. Talking shop would also overcome the temptation — every time there was a lull in the conversation — to tell Blair what he really thought of her.

'My team will be assigned another case, which could be anything from intelligence gathering for a potential murder investigation like this, to something far more mundane, like looking into suspicions about the unauthorised use of commercial premises.'

'Is that what gets your pulse racing? Murders and serious crime?'

'Are you asking if I'm like the A&E

doctors who get a buzz of excitement when the phone rings, to let them know that someone clinging between life and death is on the way into their department?'

'You watch too much TV.' He laughed at the look on her face.

'Huh! Okay, just tell me you don't get a kick of adrenaline when something like Johnny's allergic reaction happens, and you have to put off checking someone's bunions for ten minutes?'

'It's not all bunions in general practice you know. Sometimes, if we're lucky, we get a suspicious rash, or a bit of lower back pain to check out.' He shook his head, still smiling at the look of indignation on her face. 'But you're right. Emergency medicine is exciting. Terrifying and thrilling all at the same time, but it's just not something I was cut out for. I suppose I like the relationship-building of general practice more than the thrill of performing an impromptu operation to save someone's life. I'd probably be a community police officer rather than a detective, if I'd ever thought about joining the police.'

'And did you? Ever think about joining the police, I mean? Or doing anything other than being a doctor.'

'No, not even when Andrew spoke about joining the police non-stop all through sixth form. I'd always known I wanted to be a doctor, and I still love it, despite the likelihood of encountering a bunion or two. What about you, did you always want to be a detective?'

'I was always fascinated by detective shows as a kid. I spent a lot of time watching TV in my room back then, mainly to get away from Dad.' She sighed, as if she wished she hadn't mentioned him. 'My favourite show was *Waking the Dead*, about a team of cold case detectives. I even thought about being a pathologist for a while. Dad would probably have approved of that slightly more. At least I'd have been a doctor of sorts, even if all my patients

would already have been dead.'
'What changed your mind?'
'The chance to escape. I set my sights on joining the Met and making a new life for myself where I wouldn't be Mr Hannah's daughter — the consultant's kid hiding out in a relatives' room, studying whilst she waited for her father to even remember she was there. I knew the nurses felt sorry for me. They'd bring me food and magazines, and even stop to chat to me for a bit when they could. When Dad's interfering in my work now, I wish I could go back to when he barely seemed to register my existence. It's what's making the appeal of returning to the Met so strong, well part of it anyway.' Blair stirred the tea that must have gone cold in her cup by now.

'Are you really thinking of going back to London?' It was like a physical blow as she nodded. But why it should matter to him, he didn't know — they'd shared one kiss, and he'd even managed to mess that up. He didn't want a relationship anyway. Scratch that, he *couldn't* have a relationship.

'It's a bit more than thinking about it. I've decided to put in for a transfer back to London as soon as I can. Dad's right, I'm not cut out for heading up a general investigation team like the one I've got here. Specialising in something is my best chance of actually getting good at it.'

'Couldn't you do that in Scotland, by joining one of the Major Investigation Teams?'

'Probably, but that wouldn't solve the problem of my father, would it? He knows far too many senior officers up here, so he'd find some way of getting involved in my life and letting me know just what a big disappointment I was turning out to be.'

'I'm sure your team will be sorry to lose you. A lot of people will be sorry to see you go.' Noah could have said he was one of them, but that would have opened the lid to Pandora's Box again, and he wasn't sure he'd be able to shut it this time. Blair Hannah was something special, but the tragedy was that she might never realise it. And even if she did, she'd be out of his life for good by then.

* * *

Evie James eased herself down onto one of the soft seats in the surgery staff room, as her husband handed Blair yet another cup of tea. Noah had briefly explained why she wanted to see them, and the four of them were now the only ones left in the surgery.

'Thank you.' Blair took the cup of tea she almost certainly wouldn't drink. She'd had more than enough tea in the last two hours to last her a week, but it would make it feel more relaxed than the four of them just staring at each other across the table, as if this was some sort of formal police interview.

'You want to know what we can tell you about Tim Kennedy and Emily Ferguson's deaths?' Alasdair took a seat next to his wife.

'That's right. The new investigation team think there's enough suspicion following Fraser Daniels' murder to look into their deaths in a bit more detail — in case there's more to them than first suspected.'

'I feel awful.' Evie twisted her wedding and engagement rings around her finger as she spoke. 'I should have noticed something when I certified Tim. But he had a few health issues, and him having a heart attack certainly didn't seem beyond the realms of possibility. He took anti-inflammatory drugs for the back pain he'd had since falling off the scaffolding when he was renovating his house. And I knew he was stressed about money, and his wife leaving him not long after the accident meant he had to give up work. They were all factors that could contribute to a heart attack, or a stroke. But he was still quite young, so maybe alarm bells should have rung a bit more.'

‘If it’s any consolation, the pathologist thought the same initially. And, when I spoke to her after Eileen’s death, she said it would be almost impossible to tell the difference. It was only the other drugs in Fraser Daniels’ system, and the obvious injection site, that made it obvious he hadn’t died of natural causes. Whoever is behind this has the expertise to know what they’re doing. But we’re not even sure yet whether Tim and Emily *were* victims, or just a coincidence.’

‘I notified Emily’s death, and it was flagged with the Procurator Fiscal’s office because she was only thirty-five and had no physical health conditions. At least not *real* ones.’ Alasdair shook his head. ‘She suffered from Munchausen’s for a long time, and she wanted treatment for every illness she read about. She was agoraphobic and suffered from health anxiety as well, so a house call to her wasn’t that unusual — although we tried to keep them to a minimum. She took a lot of over the counter medications, and at first, I thought her cause of death might be an accidental overdose. But when the pathologist said it was most likely a heart attack, I assumed that years of taking over the counter medications to excess must finally have taken their toll.'

'Did the two of them have any other connections? Or relationships with the other victims, that you know of?' Blair still just needed that one piece of evidence, something that other people might think was insignificant, but that would reveal the whole picture that finally helped put the jigsaw together.

'They were both fairly isolated and didn't mix much with anyone. That was something they had in common with Fraser Daniels, but as far as I know, none of them knew each other.' Alasdair shook his head again, but there *had* to be something and Blair wasn't giving up.

'Did they go to church or choir practice with Father Daniels, like Eileen Dawson did?'

'Tim was always terrified that his disability benefits might be taken away from him if he was seen out and about, so he pretty much lived inside the four walls of his cottage. I should have done more to help him, too.' Evie's eyes filled with tears, and Alasdair pulled her closer to him.

'No one does more for their patients than you.' Noah looked at Evie as he spoke. 'Here you are, nine months pregnant, still trying to help them when you should be taking it easy. There's only so much you can do for people, and responding to Tim's requests for home visits was more than enough. You can't be expected to fix everyone's problems, especially when they don't even accept that there are any to be fixed.'

'Noah's right, none of this is your fault, and I'm sorry that bringing all this up is making things difficult for you.' A band of tension was tightening above Blair's eyes, and she could only imagine how Evie was feeling.

'I'm sorry, I really wish there was something we could say to shed more light on this for you, but I can't think of anything that might help.' The shadows under Evie's eyes had darkened. She needed to get home, and the last thing that Blair wanted to do was cause her stress so close to the baby arriving.

'No, I'm sorry for crashing into your Friday night. Especially as there won't be too many more before the baby arrives.' Blair smiled, and handed Alasdair a card. 'But if either of you think of anything, no matter how insignificant it might seem, just give me a call, okay?'

'Of course. Let me see you out.' Alasdair went to stand up, but Noah was too quick for him.

'Don't worry, Ali, I can do it. And I'll lock up, so you two can get home.' He held the door open for Blair and she followed him out into the waiting room. Her car was in the surgery car park, where she'd moved it from the Balloch Pass Inn after they'd left the tea rooms.

'I'm sorry. Evie looks exhausted and I've made her worry unnecessarily. There was nothing she could have done differently.' Blair took the car keys out of her handbag.

'Do you ever cut yourself the same slack?' There was an intense look on his face as she shook her head. She could have lied and said that she did, but something about him made her blurt out the truth . . . about her dad, her career, almost everything. Maybe he'd missed his true calling as a detective after all. 'Well you should give yourself a break, because there's nothing you could have done differently either. No one could have got any further with this investigation than you.'

'I wish I could believe that.' Forcing a smile, she waited as he unlocked the door that led out to the car park.

'Will I see you again now that you're handing the investigation over?'

'I don't think there's any need, do you?' She couldn't help adding that last part, even though she hated herself for it. It was one last opportunity for him to say that he wanted to see her again, and that she'd misread the signals when he'd pulled away from the kiss.

'No, I suppose not.' He opened the door and she stepped outside, striding towards her car without looking back. It was over — the investigation, at least as far as she was concerned, and, with it, her reason for being in Balloch Pass. As for what had passed between her and Noah, that was over too. Although for him, it probably hadn't even begun.

10

Noah had spent the weekend looking at job vacancies in London. It was stupid, and he hadn't done anything to follow them up — especially after his promise to Evie and Alasdair about staying put now that she was on maternity leave. But the thought that he could follow Blair back to London if he wanted to made him feel better. She'd probably ask for a transfer to the NYPD if she knew what he was thinking, after a kiss that had almost certainly meant nothing to her; but having options, even if he never took them up, was something. When Katie had died, there'd been nothing more he could do for her — there were no options left, just an empty space where all his attention had been focussed, and the guilt he still couldn't let go of. Maybe he should take the advice he gave his patients so often and book some counselling. But there was only person he really wanted to speak to, and that was Katie. If there was a hereafter, was she watching him and hating him for the lies he'd told? He wasn't sure if he even wanted there to be one, because it would mean facing her again one day, and facing up to the lies he'd told. It would be too late for him to make peace with what he'd done by then — and far too late for him to tell Blair how he felt before she left. If this was his punishment, then it probably fit the crime.

'Come in.' Noah responded to the knock on the consulting room door, and looked up as a middle aged woman, in a tight red dress that showed off far more than he felt comfortable seeing, tottered into the room. She was wearing red patent high-heeled shoes, and an expression of pure agony on her face.

'It's my feet, Dr Bradshaw, they're killing me!'

'Mrs Nugent, isn't it?' Noah scanned

her notes on the screen in front of him.

'Yes and ooh, please, you've got to do something about my feet.'

'If you can slip your shoes off, I'll take a look.' Noah got up to rinse his hands and the problem was obvious as soon as Mrs Nugent had taken off her shoes, even from the other side of the room — bunions. He had to suppress a smile, thinking of Blair. It was hardly romantic to associate her with such an unglamorous condition, but he'd never be able to look at a patient with that complaint again without thinking of Blair's joke about what GPs dealt with. Thinking about her was nothing unusual, though — just lately she was always on his mind. 'Where would you say the worst of the pain is?'

'It's at the base of my big toe and along the side of my foot, and its absolute agony!' Mrs Nugent winced again. 'And it's sore on the side there, too, where the skin is all red.'

'It looks like you've got bunions on both feet, and your big toes are starting to point towards your other toes. It's usually caused by cramming your feet into pointy, high-heeled shoes.' He gestured towards Mrs Nugent's discarded footwear. 'Do you always wear shoes like this?'

'I'm an estate agent, Dr Bradshaw, and I've got to look the part. It's no good me slumping around in Ugg boots and leggings, looking like a can't-be-bothered mum on the school run. It might be comfortable, but it doesn't fit my image.' She sniffed, wincing again as he pressed against the lump on the side of her foot.

'The only real cure is surgery, but if you want to lessen the painful symptoms to avoid that, there are a few things you can do.' As he looked up at her, she pursed her lips. 'Although I don't think you're going to like it.'

'Go on.'

'My first piece of advice is to wear a low-heeled, wide shoe with a soft sole.' She was already shaking her head. 'You can apply ice packs to the foot, and take an anti-inflammatory pain killer like Ibuprofen.'

'I can manage the second two, but I am *not* giving up my shoes. A suit or a dress doesn't look the same without the right pair of shoes to set if off, and I'm a heels girl. Always have been.'

'If you elect to have surgery, your surgeon will probably suggest not wearing high heels again. But you should definitely wait a minimum of eighteen months and, even then, stick to heels under two and a half inches.'

'I'll try the ice pack and pain killers to start with, in that case.' Mrs Nugent was already cramming her feet back into the shoes, even though they were clearly causing her considerable pain. 'Eighteen months? I just couldn't do it, Doctor.'

'I'll make you a referral to a podiatrist. That way you can talk through your options, and the impact of the choices you make, with a specialist.'

'If you like. But I'm telling you now; I'm not giving up my heels.' Mrs

Nugent shut the door behind her as Noah typed up her notes. It was strange how people stuck to bad habits so often, even when they knew it was doing them harm. But he and Blair were doing exactly the same. He was hanging on to the guilt of his past, and she was making decisions because of the control her father asserted over her — both of them using it as an excuse not to change. It was easy to hand out advice, but much more difficult to act on it. Making a note to refer Mrs Nugent, he buzzed the next patient in.

* * *

'So they haven't locked you up and thrown away the key then!' Andrew laughed so hard, Noah had to hold the phone away from his ear. 'I'll have to have a word with my colleagues up in Scotland, letting you slip through their hands like that.'

'With friends like you I've no need for enemies, that's for sure!' Noah could picture his best friend on the other end of line — sitting in a glass and chrome office somewhere, snatching five minutes to call Noah in between meetings. The higher Andrew has moved up the ranks, the more meetings he seemed to have, but he sounded happy at least. It had been a long time since Noah had heard him like that, not since before Katie's death.

'I'm glad you're off the hook and I'm glad you've decided to stay up there.'

'Should I be insulted you're so pleased that I'll be at the other end of the country from you for the foreseeable future?'

'You know what I mean, Noah. You need to start moving on from Katie's death, we all do, and London isn't the right place for you to do that. We wouldn't let you, even if you let yourself.'

'How are your mum and dad?'

'They're doing better and Mum said she likes getting your postcards. It looks beautiful up there.'

'It is.' What could he say? Once upon a time — before he'd told Katie he loved her — Andrew would have been the person he turned to, to talk about Blair. He'd have made some lame joke about how the scenery wasn't the only thing that was beautiful in the Highlands, and Andrew would have urged him to throw caution to the wind and go for it. His best friend wanted everyone to find love, like he had with his wife, Mairie. But things were different now. Noah was his sister's widower — a tragic figure who had loved and lost. So no one was going to slap him on the back and tell him to go for it, least of all Andrew.

'Mum's got something else to focus on, now, and that's why I'm ringing really. I wanted to ask you a favour.'

'Okay.' Noah rolled the pen he was holding between his thumb and index finger, bracing himself for what Andrew might want to ask. He couldn't pose as the heartbroken widower for another fundraising campaign and be able to look at himself in the mirror. He'd managed it in the early days after Katie's death because he'd been genuinely devastated to lose someone he loved. But since meeting Blair, he couldn't pretend Katie had been the love of his life. She hadn't even come close. Whether Blair might have, in different circumstances, was anyone's guess. But it had been enough to remind him that some people had that — Andrew included.

'Mairie and I are having a baby in six months' time, and we couldn't think of anyone we'd rather have as godfather.'

'Oh, congratulations, mate.' Something that felt very much like a lump was forming in Noah's throat. 'I'd be honoured, but are you sure you want me to do it? I was nearly arrested for murder less than a month ago!'

'Yeah, but we both know there's no one less likely to deliberately hurt another person than you.'

'I'm not perfect, Andrew, far from it.'

'I know, but you're as close to it as

anyone Mairie and I could think of.' Andrew's voice cracked slightly. 'And I'll never forget what you did for Katie. How you made her feel.'

'Andrew, I . . .'

'Don't say it. You loved her, probably more selflessly than any of the rest of us. When she died, you were the one who felt most sorry for *her*, and the life *she'd* lost. The rest of us were just sorry for ourselves, because we'd lost her.'

'She was an incredible girl.'

'She was, and she loved you with all her heart. So I know she'd want the best for you, and I do too. That's why Scotland is the right place for you. You can meet some gorgeous red-haired beauty, and eventually me, Mairie, Mum and Dad will want to meet her too. But you need that distance to live a new life, without having to worry about us.' Andrew cleared his throat. 'And even when some poor girl agrees to spend the rest of her life with you, and you aren't my brother-in-law any more, making you the baby's godfather will keep you in the family for good.'

'That means more than you know.' Noah had to clear his throat, too. Thank goodness it was the end of the day and he was just writing up his notes. He needed some time to process at it all before he saw anyone. But it wasn't a red-head he was picturing, it was a beautiful woman with long dark hair.

'Right, let's end this then before we say something we might regret, like how much we love each other! Speak to you soon, buddy.' Andrew's booming laugh was back, but this time Noah didn't hold the phone away from his ear. Life was moving on for his friend, and maybe it wasn't too late for his to start moving on too.

* * *

'Oh thank heavens you're still here!' Evie burst into his consulting room, without knocking, just as he was dictating his last letter.

'Are you okay? Is it the baby?' Leaping up from his chair, Noah took hold of her arm. Evie's face was flushed red, but she was shaking her head.

'No, not the baby, but I've just realised who the connection might be. I was out walking, trying to get this baby to put in an appearance as soon as possible, when it came to me. But Alasdair's taken the kids to their swimming lesson and I haven't got Blair's number. I thought I might have to dial 999 if you weren't here.' Her words were coming out in a rush, and Noah was struggling to make sense of it.

'The connection? Do you mean between the four patients who died?'

'Yes, there's one person they were all seeing regularly.' Evie took in a big gulp of air. 'Aggie Green!'

'But Aggie can't do enough to help people. She's even been cleaning for Colin Hendry since his mother died, even though she must be twice his age.'

'Exactly!' Evie leant one hand on top

of his desk, too agitated to sit down. 'She cleans for Colin, she's done some housekeeping for Father Douglas since his gout got bad and she does errands for all sorts of people, including Emma Ferguson, Tim Kennedy and Fraser Daniels. They were all isolated by illness. When the post office closed, she started running some of the bits and pieces she used to sell up to people, and I've got a vague recollection of Tim telling me she even used to run his prescriptions up to him.'

'I'd better call Blair.'

'Uh-huh.' Evie grimaced. 'And you better try and call Alasdair, after that, because I think my waters have just broken.'

* * *

Noah had left a message for Blair and he was in two minds about whether to just dial 999, and get someone out to look for Aggie Green straight away. But would they take him seriously, if he said a sixty-nine-year-old woman was possibly responsible for the spate of suspicious deaths that had blighted Balloch Pass over the past few months? And something told him Blair would want to know first. She'd know how to handle it, and who to call in, so his first priority was to make sure that Evie didn't end up giving birth in his consulting room, with her husband nowhere to be found.

Luckily Alasdair was on high alert, due to the imminent possibility of Evie going into labour, and he answered his phone on the first ring.

'Hi Alasdair, it's Noah. Don't panic, but Evie's waters have broken and I think you might need to get hold of her midwife.'

'Oh wow, really?' Alasdair's voice went unusually high. 'Sorry, I'm an idiot, of course it's really happening. As if you'd make a joke about something like that. I was determined not to be one of those panicky fathers-to-be, but this is all a bit real!'

'She's fine, don't worry, and the pains don't seem to have started yet.' Noah looked across at Evie, who was nodding her head. 'So I think you've got a bit of time.'

'Okay . . . I can give Josh a ring, he's staying with us for another week so he should be able to pick the kids up from swimming, and I can come and get Evie and drive her to the hospital.'

'That sounds good. How long do you think it will take you?'

'About twenty minutes if Josh can leave straight away. As soon as I've got hold of him, I'll either head straight over or let you know. The kids don't finish their lesson for another half an hour, so if he's available, I won't have to wait until he gets here.' It was a good job the children's uncle was over for a visit; at least something was going right.

'Okay Ali, I'll keep an eye on her until you get here.' Hopefully Blair would get his message by the time Alasdair arrived, and she'd be able to tell Noah if he needed to call it in as an emergency. There was no point him rushing off to try and find Aggie anyway. What would he say if he got there? He couldn't just accuse her of murdering four people, when the only evidence they had was the fact she'd helped them all, and Evie's hunch. Even if it was her, it was hardly as if she'd been on a rampage. The deaths were spread over months, and the chances of her killing someone else, on the day he was delaying taking action, were negligible. Weren't they?

'Noah, you need to get hold of Aggie Green, see what you can find out while you're waiting for Blair. I'll be fine here until Alasdair arrives.' Evie was pulling a face again, but this time he knew exactly why — she'd started to get contractions, although she was obviously trying to hide them.

'I'm not leaving you here until Alasdair turns up. He'd never forgive me if something happened to you.'

'And you'll never forgive yourself if it is Aggie and she hurts someone else.'

'It's less likely than you ending up giving birth on your own, though.' It was hard to argue with a woman who was in labour, and she wasn't backing down.

'I'm going to give Susie a call, she can come and wait with me until Alasdair arrives, and she can probably drive us to the hospital if we need her to.' Evie was already reaching into her bag. 'See if we've got Aggie's mobile phone number on the system, so you can give her a call.'

'I could say it's about the blood test she had done and tell her something's shown up after all.' He almost hoped Aggie Green was the killer: at least that way he wouldn't get struck off for lying to a patient, and getting her to meet him under false pretences.

He caught half of Evie's conversation with their receptionist, Susie, as he looked up Aggie's number, so he knew she was on the way. Aggie's number rang and rang, finally going to a generic voicemail message, giving no idea of when she'd next be available to take a call. She was probably doing a good deed for someone right now, whilst he and Evie were jumping to ridiculous conclusions — like a pound shop version of Holmes and Watson.

'She's not answering, and I don't want to leave a message in case she realises we're on to her and does a runner.' He could hardly believe the words that were coming out of his mouth. He'd be making a citizen's arrest when he saw Aggie, as this rate. He shook his head. 'Maybe I should just wait for Blair.'

'At least go and speak to Father Douglas whilst you wait for her to ring you. See if he thinks we're making something out of nothing. It's better than just waiting around and worrying. Susie will be here any minute.'

'Are you sure?'

'Of course I'm sure. Now get going and you can be the hero of the hour.' She smiled at him, the contractions still far enough apart for her to be comfortable in between. 'Maybe then you might even get the bottle to ask her out.'

'I'm not interested in Blair. Not like that anyway.'

'Yeah right.' Evie laughed. 'And next you'll be telling me that having a baby isn't painful. It's about as believable.'

'Evie! I'm here!' Susie called out from the waiting room. Her speedy arrival was another benefit to having a receptionist who lived three doors down from the surgery.

'We're in my room.' Noah opened the door and shouted the response. With Susie's arrival, he'd run out of time to wait for Blair. He still had no real idea what he'd say to Aggie if he found her, but Evie was right, he couldn't just sit around and do nothing. She was right about something else too — even if he wasn't quite ready to admit it to Blair.

* * *

Leaving Johnny's flat, Blair slid her phone out of the glove compartment where she'd left it. She was trying to take Bill's advice and actually have a day off. But spending two hours with Johnny and not constantly checking the phone had been enough cold turkey for one day. Okay, so she was off duty, but she had to admit she wanted to know whether anything new had come in about the case, even if it was mostly in the Major Investigation Team's hands now. There were three missed calls, all from an unknown number. It would probably just be her father, trying to get hold of her on a number she didn't recognise and immediately reject. Whenever there were a series of missed calls from the same number, it was a safe bet it would be him. He had a thick skin and a level of tenacity that might be admirable in someone else.

Clicking on the icon to play her voicemails, Blair braced herself. But they were all from Noah Bradshaw — the first message telling her that Evie had made a connection between the deaths in Balloch Pass, with Aggie Green being a regularly visitor to all of them in the months before their deaths, as well as having access to Colin Hendry's place. The second message said he'd tried to get hold of Aggie to see if he could get her to come into the surgery, on the pretext of following up some test results. And the last message said he was on his way to visit Father Douglas, to see if he had any idea where Aggie might be.

She tried to return the call — the last thing she wanted was Noah getting involved. Now that the case had been handed over, the protocol would have been to pass the information to the new team and let them follow it up. But there was a chance that Noah could be putting himself in danger and, when he didn't answer the call, there was only one other thing she could do.

'Missing me already, Boss?' Johnny answered his phone on the third ring.

'I'm still outside your flat, but there's been a development with the Balloch Pass murders. Are you ready to come back to work, right now?'

'I've been ready since I got out of the hospital. What's going on?'

'Just get down here and I'll fill you in on the way. It might be nothing, but if Evie James is right about the connection between the murders, we can't really wait around to find out.'

Reaching back into the glovebox, she took out the handcuffs she kept there and stuffed them into the pocket of her jeans. There was no guarantee they'd even be able to track Aggie down, much less that she had any real involvement in the murders. But sometimes it paid to be prepared.

* * *

Blair passed Noah running down Father Douglas' driveway in the direction of the house, and she skidded to a halt a few feet away from the house, sending up a shower of gravel that narrowly missed pebble-dashing his face. She was making a habit of churning up the priest's driveway.

'I had to stop at the level crossing for a freight train, or I'd have been here ten minutes ago.' Noah said, as soon as she opened her car door. 'But I've got to admit I am glad to see you. All this racing after a suspect is a bit out of my comfort zone. I tried calling Father Douglas, but he's not answering his phone. Although I know he's not averse to an afternoon nap these days, so I'm hoping he's just not picking up. I left a message asking Aggie to call me, but I've had nothing yet.'

'I've been calling you since I got your message, and you didn't answer me either, so it must be the signal up here.' Blair's eyes met his. She didn't tell him she was worried he might try something stupid if he got to Aggie first. Heaven knows what Johnny would make of that.

'It must be, because I haven't had any calls. Shall I go and knock, or do you want me to back off?'

'I don't want to make Father Douglas too suspicious about why we're here, in case he tips Aggie off. He might not even mean to, but we need to handle it carefully.' Blair wasn't sure if she was justifying to herself why she wanted to keep Noah around, but if he had an excuse to talk to Aggie about her health, it could come in useful. 'We'll tell him we've come to see him, to see what might have triggered Johnny's allergies, and that's why you're with us. Then, if he doesn't mention Aggie, you can do what you said in the message you left me, and tell him you've been trying to get hold of her to pass on her test results.'

'I'm definitely going to get struck off if she's innocent, telling him something like that.' Noah laughed. 'Will you give me a job if I do?'

'I'll put in a good word for you!'

Noah turned back towards the house. Walking behind him, Blair motioned for Johnny to follow suit, and the three of them stood on the doorstep as Noah rapped the big brass door knocker against the wood. There was no response.

'I'm going to look through the window and see if he's fallen asleep by the fire.' Johnny stepped none-too-carefully between the plants in the flower bed below the window. If Aggie Green saw him doing that she'd be capable of committing a murder, whether or not she'd done it before. Standing on tiptoe, Johnny peered into the high windows. 'He's not there, but there's a fire in the grate that looks like it's about to die out, so he can't have been gone long.'

'Shall we take a look around the back? He's getting a bit deaf, and if he's sitting out in the kitchen, he might not hear us.' Noah turned — he was suddenly only inches away from her, and all she could do was nod.

'You don't think anything could have happened to the old guy do you?' Blair jumped at Johnny's voice behind her.

'I doubt it, but now we're here we've got to check it out.' Blair shivered — she had a sense of foreboding, like someone walking over her grave. 'Can one of you look through the window in the back door? I think that must lead into the kitchen.'

'I can do it.' Noah answered her first, and he was already level with the door. Half a second later he caught his breath, turning around to look at Blair and Johnny. 'He's in there, tied to a kitchen chair, and Aggie looks like she's making a cup of tea.'

'Is he still alive?' Blair was almost whispering now. If they spooked Aggie, it might be too late before they could get to Father Douglas.

'His eyes are shut, but I think I can still see his chest moving.'

'Let's go back round to the front.' Blair caught hold of Noah's sleeve, and pulled him towards her so she didn't have to raise her voice. 'We can't let Aggie know we're here; we've got to find some other way into the house.'

They moved around to the front, one behind the other, like the most out-of-step conga line the world had ever seen.

‘I still can’t believe it’s Aggie.’ Noah shook his head as they got back to the front door. But nothing surprised Blair any more. She’d seen little old men, and innocent looking children, arrested for crimes that would keep most people awake at night. So the concept that Aggie Green was behind four murders, in a quiet Scottish town, was sadly all too believable.

‘That window up on the first floor is partially open.’ Blair pointed up to one of the Georgian sash windows, which was open just wide enough for someone to slip through.

‘I’d offer, Boss, but Vicky’s been feeding me up whilst I’ve been off.’ Johnny rolled his eyes, and she had to admit he was looking a bit less lean.

She turned to Noah. ‘And you’ll never get your shoulders through, either.’ He was slim, but well-built, and the last thing she wanted was him getting himself wedged, half-in and half-out of the window. If that didn’t end up alerting Aggie to their presence, nothing would. 'So it looks as if it's down to me.

'I think I can climb up the trellis, if you can give me a leg up to grab hold of it?' Noah nodded in response and he hoisted her up with apparent ease. If he'd groaned at the shock of her weight, she hadn't heard it. She just hoped the trellis was as secure as it looked.

'Be careful.' Noah spoke in a loud whisper, but she didn't respond. Moving slowly up the trellis and getting through the window intact was her only priority. Turning her head on one side, she reached out and grabbed the internal window sill — pulling her body in behind her. The window sill was very low to the floor in the upstairs bedroom she found herself in, and there was a thick rug just below it which meant she didn't make much noise as she scrambled through. All she had to do was get downstairs without Aggie hearing her, and they'd be home free.

Taking her shoes off, she gingerly stepped down the stairs, holding her breath on each new tread, in case that was the one that made the old wooden boards creak beneath her feet.

The heavy oak front door was on the latch and she lifted it, opening the door slowly, and beckoning for Noah and Johnny to come inside.

'We need to take Aggie by surprise.' She was still whispering, as they moved slowly past the staircase towards the kitchen. 'If you grab her arms, Johnny, I can restrain her and Noah will be free to see if Father Douglas is okay.'

'Yes, Boss.' Only Johnny answered, but his job was the priority anyway. If it was already too late to help Father Douglas, it didn't matter how quickly Noah acted — and the possibility hung in the atmosphere.

'Here we go.' Blair turned to the others as they reached the door of the kitchen. She counted down with her fingers — three, two, one. Flinging the door open, for a moment everything seemed to go into slow motion. And then all hell broke loose.

* * *

Aggie Green turned and grabbed a knife out of the block on the work surface in front of her. There was a wild look in her eyes that Noah had only ever seen a few times before, when he'd been working in A&E in the early days of his career, and those patients had ended up needing to be sectioned. Instinct kicked in as Aggie lunged towards Blair, and he held his arm up to block the path of the older woman's aim, barely feeling the blade slice through the skin because of the amount of adrenaline racing through his body.

'I'm going to finish this!' Aggie screamed again, as Johnny shot past Noah, taking hold of her arms and twisting them until she dropped the knife. Seconds later Blair had her cuffed, Aggie's body writhing to and fro, like a landed fish gasping for air.

Confident that they had Aggie under control, Noah turned towards Father Douglas — his skin was grey, but he was definitely breathing. 'He's got a pulse. It's a bit fainter than I'd like it to be, but I don't think she's given him anything deadly, or he'd be arresting by now.'

'I just needed five more minutes!' Aggie was still shouting. 'I was making my peace with God.'

Blair looked over at Noah as she linked an arm through Aggie's, whose hands were cuffed behind her back, with Johnny on the other side.

'Are you okay?' There was blood pouring down Noah's arm, but he nodded in response, grabbing a tea towel to stem the flow.

'I'll be fine, it's just a flesh wound.'

'It might have been a lot different if she'd got to me first. Thank you.' She gave him a small smile, and he felt it — this was a life changing moment. Not just because it was something he'd remember until the day he died, but because it was a reminder that life was too short not to take a chance sometimes. Taking a chance had saved Father Douglas' life, and it might just save Noah's too.

11

Blair smoothed down a non-existent wrinkle on the front of her shirt and took a deep breath. Aggie Green was waiting in the interview room, and DCI Booth, who was heading up the Major Investigation Team, had asked her to be part of the interviewing team with him.

'Are you ready for this?' DCI Booth put his hand on the interview room door, and turned to her.

'Absolutely.' She was more than ready to face the woman who'd been prepared to stab her in a final desperate attempt to escape justice. Blair had expected Aggie to be deemed unfit for interview, but she'd calmed down within minutes of being arrested, and the police doctor had confirmed that she was fit for detention and questioning. So this was it, the chance to find out what was behind it all, or for Aggie to simply say ‘*no comment*’ to every question asked, as so many suspects did. It was now or never for Blair, either way.

DCI Booth recorded the legal introduction for the tape and asked Aggie to confirm her details. She had a strangely serene expression on her face, and Blair’s scalp prickled, in the way it always did when she felt uneasy.

‘I know you’ve been asked this already, but are you sure you don’t want any legal representation before we start the interview?’ DCI Booth gave Aggie a few seconds, but she just shook her head. ‘Can I ask you, for the benefit of the tape, to confirm that you don’t want legal representation?’

‘That’s right. I just want to get this over with now.’ Aggie looked directly at Blair. ‘The game’s up, thanks to that young woman sitting next to you. So we may as well just get on with it.’

‘Are you saying you want to make a confession?’ Blair couldn’t believe it would be that straightforward and the new team were already looking into whether there might be more than four murders. Aggie looked so normal — nice even. But then criminals didn't come with their crimes stamped across their foreheads, and Blair would be out of a job if they did.

'I'll tell you what happened, if that's what you mean. Starting with Emily Ferguson and then the rest.'

'Were there others before Emily Ferguson?' Blair glanced at DCI Booth as she asked the question, and he gave a subtle nod.

'Let's just deal with what you think you know for now, shall we?' Aggie gave her a small smile. 'I think that should be more than enough for one day.'

'You knew Emily Ferguson, then?' DCI Booth spoke in a softer voice than usual, which was almost certainly a deliberate ploy. Blair just wanted answers though, whilst Aggie was willing to give them. There was no guarantee she'd continue to talk.

'Aye, I knew her, I helped her out too.

A lot. She was a terrible hypochondriac in my opinion, always complaining about some health issue or another, but I suppose she was unwell in a way.' Aggie paused, and tapped the side of her head. 'Up here.'

'And so you visited her a lot, had access to her house?' Blair leant forward slightly, trying to see something in Aggie's face that might betray her as a cold-blooded murderer.

'I used to get her bits of shopping and collect her prescriptions for her, especially after the post office shut.' Aggie wrinkled her nose. 'But she was ungrateful.'

'What do you mean, ungrateful?' DCI Booth was still using a soothing tone that Blair couldn't get used to.

'She wasn't there for me when I needed her, not even after all the help I'd given her. Can you believe it?' Aggie grimaced. 'I asked her to sign the petition to get the post office reopened, but she said she couldn't put her name and address to it. Because she wouldn't be able to cope if someone got in touch afterwards and asked her to explain why she signed the petition. She said that was too much to ask of her.'

'And that made you angry?' DCI Booth asked the question, but the expression on Aggie's face was answer enough. Her eyes seemed to go several shades darker, just talking about what had happened.

'I was angry, but most of all it made me wonder what the point of her life was. If she couldn't do something as simple as sign a petition, then what good was she to anyone?'

'So you killed her?' Blair's question was direct, and Aggie nodded. 'For the benefit of the tape, can you confirm that you killed Emily Ferguson?'

'Aye, I killed her. I injected her with potassium chloride. I told her it was a flu jab, that the pharmacy had recommended it when I picked up her prescriptions, and that I'd been trained to administer the jab. I've been a volunteer first aider at events in the town for years. So it wasn't difficult to convince her and the others that I'd been trained to do that to help the housebound and elderly, and make sure they didn't miss out on their flu jabs.'

'The others? Do you mean, Tim Kennedy, Eileen Dawson and Fraser Daniels?' Blair looked directly at Aggie again, but she shook her head.

'Not Fraser, no, but Eileen and Tim. Eileen was one of my best friends, and she'd been collecting signatures for me for the petition and everything. But then she suddenly said out of the blue that I should leave it and get on with my life. She said she'd decided to move nearer her son and grandchildren. So she was just leaving me to it, abandoning me when I needed her most.'

'And she paid for that with her life?' DCI Booth's voice had lost its softness. There was no doubting now what they were dealing with. Whether she was bad or mad was for someone else to determine. But she was definitely a serial killer.

'I told her she'd need the flu jab if she was going to be spending all that time with her grandkids and all the germs they pick up from school. She was happy to let me do it, and I chose the injection sites really carefully for all of them, to make sure they wouldn't be obvious.' Aggie smiled, and Blair shivered, despite the warmth of the interview room. 'So that first aid training didn't go to waste after all.'

'And did you kill Tim for the same reason?' Blair kept her gaze fixed on Aggie, who was still smiling.

'Not exactly. He did sign the petition, but he kept saying his life wasn't worth living, after he hurt himself and his wife left him. I got fed up with him banging on about it in the end, so I thought I'd help him get what he wanted. He was a bit like Emily really, no good to man nor beast.'

Blair could almost feel DCI Booth's back stiffening next to her. Aggie's staggering lack of empathy was breath-taking, whatever issues were behind that, and it had made her more than capable of murder.

'And what about Eileen's will, why did you change that to favour Dr Bradshaw and Father Douglas?' Aggie shrugged in response to Blair's question.

'At the time I was thankful to Father Douglas for all he'd done for me, and nothing was ever too much trouble for Dr Bradshaw. I thought they both deserved a reward and I was never interested in the money.' Aggie shrugged again. 'I thought it might make Colin Hendry a suspect, too, which would have done me a favour. It's not like he has much of a life to speak of. So if he'd ended up in prison, it wouldn't have been any great loss. I planted the typewriter I used in his house when I was cleaning, and it didn't take you and your sidekick long to work out it was the one used for Eileen's will.'

'But then you killed Fraser Daniels?' Blair paused. Aggie had said his death was different, and it was the one that had left them in no doubt they were dealing with murder. She wanted to know what had changed — what had gone wrong and caused her to make such a drastic mistake?

'Aye, I killed him. I went out to see him to ask if he would write a letter to support the campaign and talk about how a local post office was so important to people like him. He said no, and we got into a bit of row.' Aggie sighed. 'I should have kept my temper until after the injection. But when I offered it to him, he said no to that too. He said he didn't want to take any medication he hadn't been prescribed, while the inquiry into Eileen's death was going on. He told me he'd even refused to let Dr Bradshaw in to see him, so I knew this one would have to be different. I made us a pot of tea with the plan of talking him round, telling him he could trust me. But then he started talking about how Eileen, Tim and Emily had all been friends of mine, and wasn't it funny how they'd all died out of the blue. I laughed the coincidence off, and made us another cup of tea, but I put Rohypnol in his.'

'And it was after that you gave him the injection?' DCI Booth widened his eyes.

'Aye, but he wasn't fully unconscious, and that's when he tried to fight me off. That's why the injection got botched, and he was obviously bruised. I knew then that it was only a matter of time before someone,' she looked at Blair again, 'pointed the finger at me.'

'And that's when you decided to kill Father Douglas, too?' That was the one thing Blair still couldn't work out — Aggie had seemed devoted to the priest, yet she'd been willing to murder him.

'First I decided to give you something else to think about, in the hope that it might throw you off the trail. I bought some almond milk for that sidekick of yours, knowing that when you showed up again, I could slip some in his tea and get rid of you both. I was in the kitchen at Father Douglas' house when you turned up, but he thought I'd left for the day, so I knew he'd be making the tea. I changed the milk over and hid outside the back door while he was putting everything on the tray. When he went back into the drawing room, I riffled through the coats he'd hung up in the hallway, found the allergy injection and stuffed it down the back of the radiator, before slipping outside the front door to watch it all unfold from behind the bushes.' Aggie actually laughed this time. 'The look on your face when you were bringing him out of the house was priceless, and I knew it would buy me enough time to tie up the rest of the loose ends.'

'But why did you want Father Douglas dead?' It was just as well DCI Booth asked the question, as Blair was using all her energy not to fly at Aggie for putting Johnny's life in danger like that.

'I did it because he was leaving me

too. He was retiring and he told me that I should stop fighting to get the post office back, just like Eileen. If he was going to leave me, then I was going to make sure he was leaving this world, as well, and that I'd be leaving it not long after him. But I couldn't do it, at least not as quickly as with the others. I put Rohypnol in his tea, like with Fraser, and I tied him to the chair in the kitchen, where we'd been sitting talking before the drugs kicked in. But because it was Father Douglas, I needed to make my peace with God before I did it. I was making more tea, so I could sit and talk to Him, to explain why I was sending Father Douglas up there early.' Aggie pointed towards the ceiling 'And why I was going to follow him, despite what the church says about that being a mortal sin. But then you lot burst in and I wanted to stop you all, just until I'd finished what I needed to do.'

'So that's when you came at DI Hannah with a knife?' DCI Booth inclined his head towards Blair as he spoke.

'I just wanted long enough to finish off the job. To take me and Father Douglas out of the picture for good, that's all.'

'And are you having suicidal thoughts now?' Blair didn't want her trying anything; justice needed to be served.

'No. All the time Father Douglas is still here, I will be too.'

'Was someone else in on all this with you? You had to be getting hold of the potassium chloride somehow.' DCI Booth was pushing forward with the next stage of his team's investigation. And he'd already briefed Blair that they'd be pursuing other lines of inquiry, to make sure no one else needed to be charged in connection with the deaths.

'You can get anything on the internet if you know where to look.'

'But no one knowingly supplied you with drugs for a criminal purpose?' DCI Booth wasn't giving up that easily.

'No comment.'

'And are there any other crimes you'd like to disclose to us now, before we end this interview?' DCI Booth looked as though he already knew the answer.

'No comment.'

'In that case, we'll terminate the interview there, at eleven fifty three.' DCI Booth pressed the stop button on the recording, and Blair massaged her temples. That was it; her part of the investigation was over with. Apart from a possible online supplier, it looked as if Aggie had acted alone. Luckily Father Douglas was recovering well, and Noah's wound wasn't serious. It was up to the Major Investigation Team and the Procurator Fiscal to decide what happened next, but at least Blair could walk away feeling like she'd done her job. She just had to decide exactly how far walking away would take her.

* * *

'Can I have a word before you go, Blair?' DCI Booth called from the other end of the corridor, just as Blair was about to push through the double doors to freedom.

'Of course. Do you want me to come to your office?' She turned and walked back towards him.

'No, it's fine. I just wanted to ask you something.'

'Okay.' If he thought she'd done something wrong in the interview, she'd take it on the chin. The most important thing was that they'd got a result.

'I wanted to ask if you're still planning on going ahead with the transfer back to the Met? The Superintendent doesn't want to lose you, and neither do I. So I wondered if I might be able to persuade you to join one of the Major Investigation Teams, preferably mine.'

'That's an amazing offer, can I think about it?'

'Of course.' DCI Booth smiled. 'Just make the right decision, okay?'

'I will.' He nodded in response, and turned back towards the double doors at the other end of the corridor, which led to his office. Blair's mind was whirring as she headed out of the building and got inside her car. Flattering as it was to be asked, was joining a Major Investigation Team really what she wanted? She just wasn't sure anymore.

Picking up her phone, there were two texts.

From Father

I hear you proved me wrong and made a success of that investigation after all. It's the talk of the club. I know you don't want my approval, but maybe you need to hear this. Your mother would be so proud of you. So perhaps you should carry on doing what you've always done, and ignore this old man, and maybe I should try and remember how little I know about what you do. I'd like to change that, though, Blair. I'm ready whenever you are.

From Noah Bradshaw

Evie and Alasdair had a baby girl and, guess what? They're going to call her Hannah, as they want her to grow up to be a strong woman, like a certain DI Hannah they know! I'll be with Alasdair and a few others wetting the baby's head at the Balloch Pass Inn at lunch time, if you get a chance to pop over. If not, maybe give me a call when you're free, there's something I need to tell you X

Blair read the second message through her tears. The mention of her mum was almost always enough to start her off, but it was the closest her father had ever got to saying sorry, and that was what had really got to her this time. Maybe, just maybe, there was a chance for them to build a different, less toxic relationship. And maybe putting some distance between them, and relocating to London to re-join the Met would help with that. Whatever happened next, it was a huge leap forward from where they'd been a week before.

Finding out that Evie and Alasdair were naming their baby Hannah, even if it was really just a coincidence, made her cry even more. Whatever Noah had to say, she was ready to hear it, and it might even make her decision about going back to London a bit easier. She wanted the chance to say thank you to him, too, for believing in her when she'd been so close to giving up. Whatever happened, he'd played a part in changing her life and finally making her stand up to her dad, and she'd always be glad she'd met him.

* * *

'I can't believe how beautiful she is, Noah! Even her little fingernails. How can something that tiny be so perfect?'

'If you weren't a doctor, Ali. I might try and explain it to you.' Noah clapped his friend on the shoulder and laughed. For a brilliant GP, Alasdair seemed to be having real trouble getting his head around the miracle of life, now that it had happened to him. He looked at the picture on Alasdair's phone again. 'She is absolutely perfect, though, you're right, and I can't wait to meet her in person.'

'They're hoping to let Evie and the baby out tonight. But I'm going to get the kids as soon as Josh brings them back from the cinema, to take them to see the baby, just in case they decide to keep Evie in.' Alasdair had looked at his watch every five minutes since he'd arrived at the pub, and had stuck to orange juice to celebrate the arrival of his daughter.

'How do you think the kids will be about having a new addition to the family?' Should he have said sister? It was tricky to know, given that Alasdair was actually their godfather. But they seemed so blended as family — in the end it probably didn't matter what labels they used. It was just about love.

'They can't wait. Bronte's been asking every day since we told her that Evie was having a baby whether she'd be arriving that day! I can't wait to see their faces when they finally meet her, and we all get to be together.'

'I've got to admit I'm a bit envious.'

'I know losing Katie was hard, but you'll get there, Noah, just give it time. Talking of which,' Alasdair looked towards the door of the pub and then down at his watch again, 'I think it's about time I headed back to the house to meet Josh and the kids. But someone else has just turned up who can keep you company.'

'Congratulations!' Blair kissed Alasdair on the cheek, as she got to the bar. 'I love the name, by the way.'

'Me too. Funny thing is, we couldn't agree on one. But we were talking about you and the case at the hospital, and Evie said 'What about Hannah?'.' Alasdair grinned. 'It just seemed right somehow. After all, we couldn't very well go for Blair. It might make things complicated if you and Dr Bradshaw here finally . . . '

Noah dug him in the ribs before he could say anything else. 'Haven't you got to go and meet, Josh?'

'Right, I have. Well, hopefully we'll see you again soon, Blair. And if you want to pop by and meet your namesake, you'd be more than welcome.' Alasdair hugged them both and then worked his way out of the pub. People were stopping to shake his hand as he passed — news of the baby's arrival was spreading fast.

'Is it always like this in here on a Saturday, with you doctors treated like local celebs?' Blair laughed, and he fought the urge to take hold of her hand and blurt out everything he wanted to say. But if he did that, she might even beat Alasdair out of the pub.

'I think it's the excitement about the new baby. Anyway, if people knew you were the detective who'd made Balloch Pass a safe place to live again, you'd be the one getting handshakes and high fives. Can I at least get you a drink to celebrate?'

'Are you taking the mickey, Dr Bradshaw? I can't even claim to have taken out the pensioner who was behind all this singlehandedly.' She smiled. 'In fact, seeing as you saved me from getting stabbed, I think I'm the one who owes you a drink. What will it be?'

'If you put it like that, I'll have a whisky and soda.'

'Coming right up. See if you can grab us a table and I'll bring it over.'

There were three empty tables in the far corner of the bar, away from where everyone else was sitting and chatting — the main topics of conversation no doubt the arrival of baby Hannah, and Aggie Green's arrest. Noah tried not to make it obvious that he was watching Blair as she walked back towards him, but at least he'd stopped trying to fool himself. He'd practised what he wanted to say the night before with Stanley the dog, who was now a permanent fixture in his cottage.

'So what was it you wanted to tell me?' Blair set the drinks down on the table in front of them and, like Alasdair, she seemed to be sticking to orange juice. She probably had somewhere she needed to go, maybe even someone she needed to go there with. But if he didn't say it now, he never would. If Andrew's phone call, and everything that had happened in Balloch Pass over the past few weeks, had made him realise anything, it was that life was for the living. Katie would have wanted that for him, whether she'd known the truth about how he felt or not, and he did too.

'I wanted to tell you I've been hoping things might have changed, now you've solved the case, and made you realise you don't need to go back to London. There are people who need you here. People who *want* you here.'

'Like who?' Instead of sitting opposite him, she sat down on the bench seat beside him, her leg brushing against his.

'People like me.'

'People *like* you?' She was the one teasing him now, but he deserved it after pulling away from that kiss, when all he'd wanted to do was kiss her back. If she was going back to London, then he wasn't going to miss his chance again.

'Okay, not people like me. *Me*. I want you to stay.'

'Because you'd feel safer if I was around to keep an eye on the mean streets of Balloch Pass?'

'No, because I'd miss you if you were six miles away, never mind six hundred.'

'And if I kissed you again, Dr Bradshaw. Would that make *you* run a mile?'

'Maybe we should finish these drinks and find out.' He finally took hold of her hand. 'I messed up before because I had it my head that I'd be letting Katie down by giving myself the chance of being with someone who I could possibly fall in love with. For real.'

'And now you're ready to take that chance, whether it turns out to be love, or a big, fat mistake?'

'I'm ready, however it turns out. But if you're leaving, or you're not interested, you better tell me now so I can get every one of my patients in here to buy me a drink, to drown my sorrows.'

'I'm not leaving. I got offered a job with one of the major investigation teams, but I decided on the drive over here to stick with the job I've got. You made me realise that the only person I should be trying to please is myself. I took the job because I wanted to head up my own team, and I think we've done alright so far.' Blair squeezed his hand.

'You certainly have, and what about dating a local doctor, is that something you can see yourself doing?'

'I'm willing to give it a try, on one condition.'

'What's that?'

She grinned as she looked at him. 'As long as you promise never to offer me a do-it-yourself flu jab!'

'I can promise you that! Come on, let's get out of here. I made a promise to Stanley, too, to take him out for a long walk if I managed to persuade you to date me. He's been helping me work out how to say the right thing, and he's a very good listener!' Pulling her to her feet, there was a lot more he wanted to promise. But, as Alasdair had said — if things turned out right — all that would come in time.

Getting involved in a murder investigation was something he could never have imagined, but it had given him the *chance* of finding real love for the first time in his life. And for now, that was more than enough.

We do hope that you have enjoyed reading this large print book.

Did you know that all of our titles are available for purchase?

We publish a wide range of high quality large print books including:
Romances, Mysteries, Classics
General Fiction
Non Fiction and Westerns

Special interest titles available in large print are:
The Little Oxford Dictionary
Music Book, Song Book
Hymn Book, Service Book

Also available from us courtesy of Oxford University Press:
Young Readers' Dictionary
(large print edition)
Young Readers' Thesaurus
(large print edition)

Other titles in the
Linford Romance Library:

MELTING EVIE'S HEART

Jill Barry

Film-set director Evie is between projects, and hurting from being dumped by the arrogant Marcus. Escaping to spend Christmas in her parents' idyllic countryside home, what will finally lift her mood — her mum's relentless festive spirit, the cosiness of village traditions . . . or the attention of gorgeous antiques dealer Jake? When the leading duo in this year's village pantomime drops out after a bust-up, Evie and Jake are roped in to take over. But with Evie playing the princess, just how seriously will Jake take his new role as Prince Charming?

LOVING LADY SARAH

J. Darley

As life returns to normal after the war, Lady Sarah Trenton's reality is put into perspective. Her love for Robert, the gamekeeper's son who has returned home safely, is as alive as ever. But they must meet in secret, for Lord Trenton, whose heart has been hardened by the loss of his son, intends to see his daughter marry a man of wealth and status — like the odious Sir Percy. The times are changing, but the class divide is as wide as ever. Will Sarah and Robert be forced apart?

FORBIDDEN FLOWERS

Alice Elliott

An embarrassing slip in the Hyde Park mud leads Lily and Rose Banister into the path of Philip Montgomery, a British Embassy diplomat. Mesmerised by Lily's beauty, he invites her to accompany him to the Paris Exhibition, while Rose, who can't help but feel envious, is asked to chaperone the trip. Arriving in Paris, the trio happen upon Philip's old adversary Gordon Pomfret, who decides to join their group, obviously vying for Lily's attention. Meanwhile, Rose and Philip discover that their shared interests might just make them kindred spirits . . .

CLOSE TO THE EDGE

Sheila Spencer-Smith

Grieving the death of her brother, Alix decides to make a fresh start on the Dorset coast. Her new job, running the tearoom attached to Mellstone Gallery, comes with its own difficulties — not least the petulant attitude of her employer's daughter Saskia. On top of this, Alix soon discovers the feud between her landlady and her neighbours, twins Cameron and Grant. Despite being warned to stay away, Alix is drawn to Cameron's warm nature. With his plans to move north and her turbulent past, could they have a future together?

SILENCED WITNESS

Tracey Walsh

Morven Jennings is a super recogniser: she has the ability to remember the faces of almost everyone she's ever seen. Having lived under an assumed identity in witness protection since the murder of her parents when she was sixteen, she hopes one day to spot the face of the killer in a CCTV image. But when her investigation of the abduction of a baby from Heathrow Airport takes her down unexpected avenues, it brings shadows of her past to light — and puts her in the sights of dangerous enemies . . .